The
PETTICOAT PARTY

Phoebe's Folly

The
PETTICOAT PARTY
Book 2

Phoebe's Folly

KATHLEEN KARR

HarperCollins*Publishers*

Library of Congress Cataloging-in-Publication Data
Karr, Kathleen.
    Phoebe's folly / Kathleen Karr.
        p.   cm. — (The Petticoat Party ; bk. 2)
    Summary: Now armed with rifles, the self-reliant women of the Petticoat
Party wagon train continue on their journey to Oregon City and face more
challenges, including a shooting contest with a band of Snake Indians.
    ISBN 0-06-027153-1. — ISBN 0-06-027154-X (lib. bdg.)
    [1. Sex role—Fiction.   2. Overland journeys to the Pacific—Fiction.
3. Women—West (U.S.)—Fiction.]   I. Title.   II. Series: Karr, Kathleen.
Petticoat Party ; bk. 2.
PZ7.K149Ph   1996   96-15642
[Fic]—dc20   CIP
                                                                      AC

Typography by Steve Scott
1   2   3   4   5   6   7   8   9   10
❖
First Edition

To Mary Lee
For sharing the long trail from college

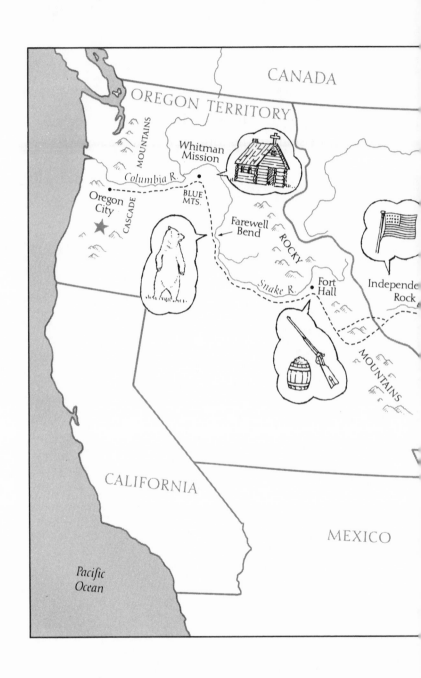

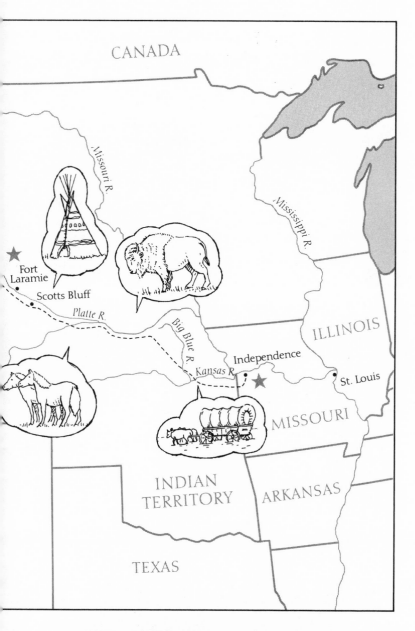

Missouri R.

Mississippi R.

Fort
Laramie

Scotts Bluff

Platte R.

Big Blue R.

Kansas R.

Independence

ILLINOIS

St. Louis

MISSOURI

INDIAN
TERRITORY

ARKANSAS

TEXAS

← THE OREGON TRAIL: 1846 →

ONE

$\mathcal{G}$unfire cut the early morning air. It was a spine-chilling, gut-tightening sound, even though I was standing right next to it. A person of some imagination might easily figure that the ten thousand Sioux camped nearby were on the warpath.

But no. This gunfire was just outside the western walls of Fort Laramie, far enough from the Indian camp to the east. We, the members of Miss Simpson's Petticoat Party, were laying over an extra day, and the scruffy, teasing men from the fort had set up a shooting range for the edification of us females. Considering as how we'd turned up at Laramie just two days earlier, with only our reputation for survival preceding us, it was downright gallant and charitable of them.

Not that any of us females had asked for charity, or even expected it. We'd made it this far across the plains on our own steam, hadn't we? We'd been on our own for a long time, ever since that disastrous buffalo massacre hundreds of miles back on the trail. An unforgettable hunt *that* had been, with the buffalo ending up stampeding our men, instead of the other way around. The beasts had spared only four—and those four, like Papa with his broken legs, not one whit of use to us remaining womenfolk.

We'd made it without gunpowder or even knowing how to shoot a rifle. That's what had truly shocked the hunters and wilderness men inside Laramie. There were still fourteen hundred miles to trek before Oregon, though. Maybe the males at the fort figured our ghosts would come back to haunt them if we all expired along the way from not knowing how to shoot some food.

I studied our outlandish teachers with new feelings of benevolence in my heart. Men could be useful creatures when they set their minds to it.

"It's your turn, Phoebe!"

"Thank you, Amelia." The family rifle was suddenly in my hands. I hoisted it to my shoulder just like my big sister had, and squinted down the long barrel. I wasn't absolutely certain I was cut out for this kind of thing.

"See the whiskey jug jest restin' on that rock, missy?"

"Yes, sir, Mr. Harley."

"Well, that there is your settin' rabbit. Now, you

got to keep in mind, rabbits don't set very long. Ain't no wildlife does. It's agin their health and natures. You got to shoot while the shootin's good."

"Yes, sir, Mr. Harley." The rifle was getting heavy. The barrel began to tremble as I reached for the trigger. I whispered a quick prayer, shut my eyes, and squeezed. The recoil knocked me clear back into the arms of Mr. Harley behind me. I was fairly sure I'd missed, but cast my eyes in the direction of the hunter's unshaven face for verification.

Mr. Harley gave a mournful shrug. "There'll be an empty stewpot over the fire tonight, missy."

"Thought as much." Struggling out of his odoriferous embrace, I picked up the fallen gun. I wasn't quite ready for another shot. "Maybe if we went over the loading procedure again . . ."

"Wouldn't hurt none, missy. But first we got to get that dirt from the barrel. You clog a barrel so, next thing you know that rifle'll blow up right in your pretty little smudged face. And not that mop of bay-colored hair nor even those bright green eyes'll save you. Always was partial to bay. My favorite old nag, Hortense, was a bay."

Pretty? All Mr. Harley's compliments save that one went clear past me. I scowled as I wiped black powder from one cheek and shoved some of that wild auburn hair behind an ear. There was no way I could be considered the pretty one of the wagon train. A nearly thirteen-year-old female was never *pretty*. That word had to be reserved for my dark-haired sister, Amelia, standing off to one side of me. Seventeen she was, and distinctly pretty since she'd shed most of her excess fat along the last six hundred hungry miles of trail. Or the word applied to the pertly freckled, carrot-headed O'Malley girls lining up to shoot ten feet down the staggered line of would-be marksmen. Or—I hated to admit it—the perfect, blond, blossoming Kennan twins.

Mr. Harley never even noticed the fifteen-going-on-twenty-year-old Kennans poised just past the O'Malleys. He just went through the cleaning and loading of the gun with infinite patience. It surely was remarkable how a man who didn't have enough sense to wash or shave could take such good care of guns.

When we were all set again, Mr. Harley paused to examine my arms. It was easy, since my sleeves were already rolled up to my elbows in the growing heat.

"Don't think you got nothin' wrong with your eyes, missy, once you learn to keep 'em open. But those arms sure could use some strengthenin' up."

I flexed the limbs in question. They'd never before seemed so puny. Hannah and Sarah Kennan didn't have that problem, either. "How would I do that?"

"When you set out on the trail again, you take to carrying a heavy sack couple hours a day. Start at about five pound and work up to ten or more. Week or two of that, the rifle won't be a burden no more."

"Thank you kindly, Mr. Harley. I'll do it." I would, too, but in the meantime I'd have to live with my infirmity. I hefted the rifle again. The jug looked mighty small, and the prairie rolling off beyond mighty big. Somehow that made it hard to concentrate.

I blinked and focused on the tiny jug again. "May I shoot?"

This round I kept my eyes open the whole entire time. I still missed the jug, but not by all that much. Mr. Harley was pleased enough.

Amelia took her turn and actually winged the jug. She let out an unladylike whoop, and all the girls cheered. Lizzie O'Malley was doing pretty fair too. Maybe that was because she was seventeen just like my sister. Maybe age had something to do with it. Then again, those widow women from our wagon train were struggling something fierce. On the far end of the shooting line gray-haired Mrs. Davis surely looked like she'd rather be using her plump arms for scrubbing at laundry, and Mabel Hatch and the other younger widows were already turning teary with frustration. Happy Hawkins, Miss Simpson's second-in-command, was the only grown woman who hadn't needed lessons. Miss Prendergast's eyes were too poor to consider lessons, while Mama, Mrs. O'Malley, and Mrs. Kennan had outright refused them.

The big surprise was the twins.

Hannah and Sarah Kennan still hadn't given up their prime interest in anything male, preferably Indian male—not even after their unbelievable Pawnee adventures. They'd come incredibly close to becoming Indian squaws, and relished every moment of the experience.

Wouldn't you just know it. They'd been allotted two almost respectable-looking young half-breeds as their instructors. You could certainly pick out the Indian half in those strong noses and bronzed faces. As for the half-breeds' dress, well, it was a motley assortment of buckskin breeches and wildly dyed shirts. Finishing off this sartorial splendor, Hannah's young man had a yellow silk sash wrapped around his waist, while Sarah's sported purple ribbons entwined in his long black pigtails. It was apparent the two educators were enjoying their pupils, too. Yet the constant flash of white teeth didn't seem to interfere with their directives in the least.

How those twins were learning to shoot! It was enough to turn a red apple green again. As the hours marched by, they must have destroyed half the crockery in Fort Laramie. I progressed, too, of course, but only because Mr. Harley decided to let me give it a try from a prone position, settled flat out on the dry prairie grass. That extra bit of elbow support was what my arms needed, all right, because I managed three hits in a row by sundown. Both elated and exhausted by that point, I turned to Mr. Harley for his opinion.

"You'll do, missy." The gleam of pride in his eyes was my reward.

Gratefully, I retired the weapon for the day. "I'm much obliged, Mr. Harley. Your name will be raised when I give thanks for my first rabbit stew."

He turned courtly in his pleasure and gave me a little bow. "Couldn't think of no nicer remembrance, missy."

Miss Simpson had scheduled us to take off on the trail again the next morning. Miss Simpson believed in schedules, being a former headmistress, or at least teacher—I hadn't yet clearly figured which. She'd taken over as captain of our train directly after the buffalo disaster, when no one else had the strength to think about being in charge. Anyway, it had gotten so that when Miss Simpson made up her mind, she wasn't questioned. Maybe it had something to do with her broad shoulders and generally formidable physique. Nobody would call *her* an old maid to her face—or behind her back, either. Nobody called her anything except Miss Simpson.

But walking around the campfires that night, I could tell enthusiasm wasn't real high for leaving our temporary haven. Such as it was. I shook my head to myself. What kind of fort didn't even have a doctor to tend to our ailing men? Still, meals were being swallowed in a kind of Last Supper gloom with all eyes focused on the fading outlines of Laramie's stockades. Equipment was being checked and rechecked to make certain nothing had been forgotten that might save our lives on the next fourteen-hundred-odd miles of our journey.

Only the Kennan twins seemed to have other things on their minds. They'd stolen away from their mother and were meeting with those two half-breeds behind the farthest wagon. I noticed that, on account of the one young man's bright sash caught the moonlight almost as well as the twins' blond hair. I suppose those twins figured half-Indian was better than none at all. Their former Pawnee suitors, Panther Claw and Wind Pony, were probably well out of the entanglement.

The reason for my stroll was simple enough. I was hoping to get a final look at my little Sioux brother, Yellow Feather, whom I'd rescued from drowning back at Scotts Bluff. I fingered the scar on my palm from the blood-sister ceremony his family had given me. The cut had healed into a fine white line. It was a mark of honor; I hoped it would be with me always, along with the other memories of that magical, starlit night.

Yellow Feather and his family had to be somewhere on the other side of Laramie, in that great encampment of thousands of Indians. Already the drums were going strong, filling the prairie night with sounds that were becoming strangely comforting to me. Alas, the meeting was never meant to be. Amelia caught up with me.

"Mama wants to know where you think you're going, Phoebe."

"Just over to have a look at the Sioux—"

My big sister caught my arm. "Really, Phoebe. You're becoming as daft as those Kennan twins."

"So you saw them with their young men, too?"

"Indeed." Amelia grinned. "But not for long. I'm not sure how, but Miss Simpson got wind of it.

She was striding forth for battle when Mama sent me to fetch you."

It would be Miss Simpson doing Mrs. Kennan's dirty work again. The twins' mother never had been particularly competent to begin with, but since the death of Captain Kennan—her husband and our first leader—she seemed fit for nothing but swooning. I cringed at the thought of Miss Simpson striding forth after *me* for any reason whatsoever. "Poor Hannah and Sarah."

"Yes. Doomed to virtue till Oregon. Come along, Phoebe. We've got an early start tomorrow, and Papa's yelling from the wagon after you too."

I tarried a moment longer. The sounds and sights of a thousand Indian campfires filled my senses. Sending out prayers for a good life for my little brother, and a peaceful rest for his first sister's spirit, I finally turned. "I guess I'd best get back to work on Yellow Feather's elk skin tomorrow night."

In the morning we finally wended our way from Laramie amid alternate "Godspeed"s and catcalls from our benefactors of the previous day—a strange wilderness sort of chivalry. But at least they wished us well. That they still found us a curiosity was a trifle baffling. Hadn't we proven ourselves thus far? We had gotten to Fort Laramie. We had mastered the use of our rifles. Well, some of us had. A little more practice wouldn't go amiss where I was concerned.

Such attentions from the blockhouse of the fort were short-lived, however. As I craned my neck over the sides of our oxen I caught the men turning to the east. Small wonder. Just past the sleeping tipis a long wagon train was snaking into view, outlined by the rising sun.

"We've got company, Amelia."

"What?"

She'd already fallen back into the recesses of her mind as a comfort against the deadening trek to come.

"There's another party heading into Laramie. A big one."

Amelia gave her ox Bright an encouraging slap on his right flank. "We'd best make some time, then, hadn't we? There's only so much grass up ahead."

"That's the most practical thing I've ever heard you say, Amelia. Usually you've got your head off in the clouds somewhere, thinking up your stories, or something."

"After much consideration, little sister, I've decided being practical is the only way I'll make it to Oregon and my own life, where I can write down those stories." She smote Bright again.

←≪≫→

Walking with a five-pound sack of flour in hand got fairly tiring by the end of the day, even if it had been considerably lightened by smacking it at the oxen instead of my usual stick. When we camped down by Warm Springs that night I noticed a rather peculiar, floury tinge to the head oxen as I unyoked and led them to water. Margaret O'Malley—the second oldest of the four O'Malley girls, and the one my age—noticed too.

"How much did that flour cost you in Laramie, Phoebe?"

"Fifty cents the pint, Margaret."

She shook her carroty head. "Didn't know you Browns were rich enough to dust at least a quarter's worth over your oxen today."

"Tarnation." That gave me pause. It also made me give Buck and Bright an unexpected bath before scampering back to the family wagon to hide the depleted flour sack.

Tomorrow I'd substitute pebbles in my arm-strengthening bag. For a surety.

The days took on a certain dull evenness: yoking and unyoking the oxen morning, noon, and evening; walking and choking on their dust while the sun glared down with heat; preparing endless meals.

The same dry prairie was scattered with sagebrush; the same broad, muddy shallows of the Platte River were always to our right. After Fort Laramie there was nothing much to look forward to, aside from Oregon itself. Unless you figured on Independence Rock.

Way back in Independence, Missouri, we'd been warned to make that landmark by the Fourth of July. Arrive at the Rock anytime beyond the Fourth, the old-timers had said, and you could be certain sure of making bad time to Oregon— meaning after the snows had started.

Papa took to dwelling on this fact from his perch inside the wagon. I guess if you were an invalid cooped up like he was, boredom could make you dwell on anything beyond your fractured legs.

"How much time did we make today, daughter?"

"About twelve miles, Papa."

"That's not good enough. With this weather, and the Platte still giving us water, we should be making better."

"Yes, Papa. I'll tell that to the oxen."

"Insolence ill becomes you, Phoebe."

"No, Papa."

"We'd make better time if the animals didn't have to haul this cursed cherrywood dresser. We should have sold it back in Laramie. Might have gotten a couple slabs of bacon for it. At least it would have paid off some of the grief it's given me!"

I wasn't about to get started with Papa on the sore subject of his permanent wagonmate and Mama's pride and joy. "Excuse me while I help with the supper."

Along with regular run-ins of that nature with Papa, other patterns set in. Beyond the livestock to tend in the evening and the meal to fuss with, there'd be a few minutes stolen to work on *my* pride and joy, the elk skin from my blood brother Yellow Feather's first kill. Finally there was the ritual end-of-the-day footbathing with the girls in the Platte River, or whatever creek we might be nearest.

Slowly we inched our way farther west.

About five days out of Laramie, daily exercises with the pebble bag had me convinced that my right forearm was developing muscles and tendons of iron. Either that or I was stretching the limb into permanent disfigurement an inch longer than its left partner. In short, Mr. Harley and his rabbit stew were never far from my mind. But as I was aching clear up to my shoulder due to his exercises, thoughts of Mr. Harley were becoming somewhat less Christian in nature. Kinder reflections had not yet come to fruition. That would require a cooperative rabbit.

During the course of that long day of tutoring outside the walls of Laramie, Mr. Harley had given freely of his advice on the nature of the wily creatures. The conversations returned to me as I prowled the perimeter of our camp before bed, or during my occasional night guard duties.

"'Round these parts, there's whitetails and blacktails. Jackrabbits, that is, missy, tho' they's truly hares. Nope." And he'd pause to stroke his stubble. "Not at all like them cute little cottontail bunnies back East."

"You've been back East, Mr. Harley?"

"Where in thunder you think I sprung from, out here on this prairie? 'Course I come from back East. Kentucky. Used to be good huntin' there, too, but it got too civilized 'bout the time I was your age. . . . Watch where you're wavin' that rifle! *Never* aim its business end at a two-legged critter lessen you mean him harm. Loaded or unloaded."

"Yes, sir!" I lowered the muzzle of the rifle with alacrity.

"Now, where was I?"

"Jackrabbits, Mr. Harley."

"Correct. Your blacktail jack, he's all ears and legs, and tough as leather. But your whitetail, why, he can be as tasty a morsel as ever you et. And he comes in supper size. Seven, eight, even ten pound I've caught."

I whistled my admiration. "That would feed the entire family!"

"Gettin' me peckish just thinkin' on it. I'd try a little sport myself if the land hereabouts wasn't currently covered with Injuns. Won't be a jack, nor nuthin' else for miles—"

"Mr. Harley?"

"What, missy?"

"How would I go about finding one of these creatures? Once we're past the fort and the Indian encampment?"

"Why, you looks for their *form,* of course."

"Form?"

"That there's a little hollow they dig out in the grass 'neath nice, sheltering sagebrush. But mostly you jest sees 'em, has your rifle loaded, and takes a shot."

I must have looked highly dubious, because Mr. Harley proceeded apace.

"He'll run and jump, all right, if'n you miss that first shot. But by the time you're loaded again, he'll jest be hunkered down not far off, estimatin' the danger. That's when you spot 'im by an ear twitch and let go again."

Truly, Mr. Harley had made the rabbit-hunting business sound easy as pie. But I'd kept my eyes open now for days, and the only ones I saw were hopping away from our train in fright. In nine-foot-high bounds. Somehow I suspected my newfound marksmanship was not yet up to that.

Still, I remained optimistic. Each day I trotted faithfully off into the twilight—Mr. Harley had assured me that was their favorite feeding time—in pursuit. I was beginning to appreciate the merits of larger game. Game with sides almost as big as a barn wall, that didn't hop. Not that there were any of those in the environs, either. Surely there should be *something* five entire days' journey out from Laramie—

"Lands, Phoebe. What are you doing out here by yourself in the darkening night? With your rifle?"

I started, rifle at the ready, then recognized the blond head. " 'Lo, Hannah. Looking for rabbits. What are you doing?"

"Looking for something a fair piece more interesting."

"That half-breed with the yellow sash?"

Graceful fingers popped up to her mouth to cover a gasp. "How did you know, Phoebe Brown? James swore me to secrecy."

"James?" I dropped the muzzle, as per Mr. Harley's useful advice.

"Well, I know it's nowhere near as romantic a name as Wind Pony, but beggars can't be choosers."

"He really said he'd follow you?"

"He hinted he might be off this way guiding an eastern tourister by the name of Francis Parkman. Looking for the Crows, this Mr. Parkman was, not even traveling for new land. Can you imagine coming all the way out to this wilderness merely to sightsee?"

"No," I allowed. "I can't."

"Let me have that rifle a moment, Phoebe."

"What? Oh, surely."

Innocently I handed over the instrument, and innocently I stood by as Hannah raised it to her shoulder, sighted at something I couldn't even pick out, and shot.

"There." Hannah handed back the smoking gun. "Did you see it jump, Phoebe? I think I'll just go and fetch it."

"Fetch what?" Mouth agape, I watched as Hannah Kennan trotted into the darkness and returned with a rabbit. *My* rabbit.

Carrying it delicately by the ears, she wafted past me toward camp, her rear quarters sashaying in time with the snowy puff of the fat whitetail.

"A pity it's too late for supper, but it should be fresh enough for a lovely breakfast. Good night, Phoebe."

"That was *my* shot and *my* rifle, Hannah Kennan!" I yelled after her. "And what about James?"

"He'd be proud of me, wouldn't he? He seemed fond of self-reliant women." Hannah's words drifted back.

After kicking a sizable hole in the prairie, I followed.

Two

A week out of Laramie we were setting up night camp where Deer Creek trickles into the Platte, when a great hullabaloo broke out. It was over by Happy Hawkins's wagon. Naturally, everybody dropped whatever they were doing and ran, myself included.

At first I thought maybe it was Mr. Hawkins, coming back to his senses at last. He'd been wandering around like a wide-eyed, motherless child ever since his head had been clonked at the buffalo killing. But that wasn't the case at all. It was the young widow, Mabel Hatch, losing *her* senses.

I took in the wailing and hair-tearing with concern until Margaret O'Malley enlightened me.

"You might as well go and finish hobbling Blackie, Phoebe. Mrs. Hatch is going to have a baby, is all."

"But Mr. Hatch is dead!"

"Well, he wasn't when they were married up, was he? Probably five months gone, Happy said, and why in the world hadn't Mabel the sense to figure it out a lot sooner."

Margaret certainly had more experience observing this baby business than I, with her younger sisters and four-year-old brother, Timothy. Maybe that's why she wasn't overly distressed.

"I don't know, Margaret. Won't it make it awfully hard for Mrs. Hatch to keep walking her oxen?"

"Mrs. Hawkins said it shouldn't be a problem the next few months. She should know. She's got more experience at healing than any of us. Probably at midwifing, too, saints be praised. But Mrs. Hatch has got to drink more milk." Margaret sighed. "We've got the only milk cow. Sure and Timothy and the girls are looking at shorter rations."

A baby. It was a big thought. "How long does it take for a baby to be born, Margaret?"

"Phoebe Brown! Did you grow up under a cabbage leaf? I thought you came from a farm!"

"Well, of course. The lambs always arrived in the spring. Every spring—"

"Nine months, Phoebe. It takes nine months for a human lamb."

"Thank you for the clarification, Margaret. Maybe I can do the same for you sometime."

Carefully hanging on to my dignity, I furtively counted off months on my fingers. It was almost the end of June. Four more months . . . That was a relief. Why, by the end of October we'd surely be safely settled in Oregon. Having neatly solved the problem of possible complications to the journey due to Mabel Hatch's discovery, I returned to Papa's horse.

We finally parted from the Platte to hook up with the Sweetwater River. There, dead ahead of us, loomed Independence Rock, a half-mile-long lump rising out of nowhere from the flat prairie. And it appeared not a day too soon. We arrived for the nooning on the glorious Fourth of July. In honor of the occasion, Miss Simpson announced an afternoon layover. Mama headed straight for the river with grimy linens, while Amelia and I and the other girls took a detour to the Rock itself.

"Oh. Look! There are names everywhere!"

"It's a tradition, Margaret." Here's where I could finally go one better than Margaret O'Malley. She might know about babies, but *I* knew about the significance of the Rock.

Just the night before, Miss Prendergast and Zachary Judd had been discussing this very landmark. Dainty and bespectacled, Miss Prendergast was the other spinster schoolteacher of our party. She'd started out as companion to Miss Simpson, but lately had taken to looking after Mr. Judd. He was the injured bachelor blacksmith who was permanently lodged in his own wagon, just as Papa was in ours and Mr. O'Malley in his. That didn't keep Mr. Judd from taking a lively interest in all the landmarks along the way, though, through the little window cut from one side of his wagon canvas. Miss Prendergast had books to explain everything, and I'd join them of an evening for my own enlightenment.

"Everyone who travels past carves or paints their name on the Rock, Margaret, ever since the first trappers and explorers. Some even leave messages for friends coming behind. See here? This gentleman must have been a sailor. He's left an anchor for his mark."

The Kennan twins had bustled up behind us to catch the tail end of my explanation.

"Gracious. Look at all those men who've been through, Sarah! Do you suppose they're all waiting in Oregon?"

"But there aren't any Indian names here, Hannah dear."

"Indians don't bother with writing, sister. They leave their marks in other ways."

Sarah clutched at her heart evocatively. "They certainly do."

Amelia put a stop to the twins' nonsense. "It occurs to me, girls, that it's high time to add a feminine touch to this pile of stone. Something literate, perhaps . . ."

Amelia's deep, dark secret—her ambition to be a writer—was surfacing again. The farther west we got, the stronger this burden seemed to sit upon her. "While you're busy composing, Amelia," I said, "I'll fetch the axle grease. From the way that stuff clings, our names should rest here forever."

Amelia had been scratching words on Independence Rock for the longest time, but only managed to complete the first two lines of her intended work:

> *The Petticoat Party is our name,*
> *We came to seek both Land and Fame—*

I made a face as I pulled back from studying her half-finished sentiments. "I trust you're speaking for yourself, Amelia, because I just want to get there. And I'm not sure I wish to be remembered by posterity with such claptrap."

"Give a person half a chance, Phoebe. You haven't seen the rest of it."

I wasn't sure I wanted to, but as this was my sister's first opportunity since the mills in Lowell to express her literary bent, I gave in. "All right, then, let's hear it."

"You needn't act so patronizing, Phoebe." But Amelia recited by heart, nevertheless, from the beginning:

> *The Petticoat Party is our name,*
> *We came to seek both Land and Fame—*
> *All stalwart women with sensibility*
> *Who now have proven our capability.*
> *Onward, then, the staunch women trudge*
> *Through rain, snow, dust, or even sludge.*
> *We won't regret the toils*
> *When we receive our spoils:*
> *Peace from arduous labor*
> *Bread from thoughtful neighbor*
> *And land enough for all to share.*
> *We'll never rest till we get there.*

She paused hopefully. "What do you think?"

"You'll still be writing on that Rock till Christmas, is what I think!"

"But I've already painted the first two lines. How am I supposed to end it sooner?" When I merely shrugged, she added, "You have something more appropriate to say, Phoebe?"

"I certainly do. 'Oregon is our goal—if we get there whole.'"

"Phoebe, Phoebe—"

"Never mind. It's my turn for that axle grease."

I liberated the stuff from my protesting sister. After only a few minutes, I set down the implements with satisfaction. "There."

Amelia walked over to study my piece.

PHOEBE BROWN
"SWIFT FISH"
JULY 4, 1846

"That's all?"

"Yup. Straight and to the point. And I do think my Sioux name is a nice added touch."

Amelia gave me a condescending look as she fetched the axle grease and went back to her own labors. "Posterity *will* tell, Phoebe. And I intend to give it more to work with. Go play on the Rock or something, so I can concentrate."

Later, from a foothold halfway up that very Rock, Margaret and I spotted a trail of dust from the east.

"Company's coming!" I bellowed down. Then Margaret and I watched as the wagons came into focus.

The group arrived, tired, dusty, and celebratory as the afternoon wore to a close. It was a big party, of maybe fifty or more wagons. And they had no dearth of men. Men who were shortly hauling out rifles and jugs. As dusk descended, they'd swallowed enough from the jugs to keep those rifles popping off halfway into the night.

Miss Simpson stood aloof from these showier celebrations of Independence Day. Yet she certainly approved of marking the occasion; she just didn't necessarily endorse the manner in which our neighbors chose to observe it. She actually attempted to gather our people together directly after supper to give a little speech. When only a handful of us showed, due to the temptations of those "showier celebrations," Miss Simpson gave up. Another volley of shots sounded. "A waste of good gunpowder," she sniffed in dismissal.

Miss Simpson went off to sleep directly after members of the new party came to invite us to a dance. The prospects of such levity found other enthusiasts, however.

"May we go to the dance, Mama? Please?" There was a sparkle of interest in Amelia's eyes.

"Well, dear, I really cannot see why not. One only passes the Fourth at Independence Rock once in a lifetime." She shuddered as a new barrage of gunfire shattered the night. "Hopefully, that is. . . . But perhaps you ought to ask your father."

"Their father's perfectly aware of the situation," Papa barked from the wagon. "Nobody'll be getting any sleep in this ruckus. You might as well let the girls go watch, Ruth."

"Oh, thank you, Papa!"

Before he could change his mind, Amelia and I were gone.

Along with the whiskey, the newcomers had also hauled out instruments. These they were tuning by the light of lanterns strung around a big circle of wagons. In the center, couples were chatting, ready for the festivities. A single fiddle started in, to have its tune picked up by several others. The hoedown had begun.

Margaret O'Malley came running over, and the three of us stood there, tapping our toes. I wouldn't have minded doing more, but my lack of experience was too daunting. Instead, I watched as a tremendously presentable young man swaggered out of the crowd to bow dashingly before Amelia and sweep her into the fray.

"Now, where do you suppose Amelia learned how to do that? At the cotton mills in Lowell?"

"I'm not sure, Phoebe, but I think Lizzie must have taken lessons in the same place."

We watched, slightly jealous, as our big sisters capered to the music with the strangers. There were a lot of people dancing, but it gradually occurred to me that two in particular were missing. "Where are the Kennan twins, Margaret? Surely they'd enjoy this. Even if it isn't a war dance."

Margaret grinned through the darkness. "It's certain I am they would, indeed, Phoebe. If their mother hadn't dragged them both into their wagon as I walked by . . . They do protest with spirit."

"More like stuck pigs, the times I've overheard them."

Margaret snickered appreciatively before glancing at her sister again. "Maybe it's just as well."

"True. Our sisters deserve a turn."

As the first dance ended and another tune was struck, it appeared Amelia and Lizzie were getting that turn sure enough. Their young men seemed unwilling to part with them. It was only as the night grew long, and even I began to tire, that Amelia was finally returned. We wended our way back to our wagon. At least I wended. Amelia was still flying high.

"His name is Wade Jennings, Phoebe. He's bound for Oregon City. And he's a printer by trade!"

"Better come back down to earth, Amelia!"

Starry-eyed as she was, I had to keep my sister from tripping over no less than three wagon traces till I deposited her safely on the blankets Mama had set out for us. "He looked at least twenty, Amelia. Are you sure he's not married?"

"Twenty-one. And he's come all this way with only his best friend—Lizzie's partner—and a printing press." Amelia flopped onto her blankets, dreamy.

Try as I might, I could get not another syllable out of her. I slid into my own blankets with a sigh. It looked suspiciously as if another female with some promise had gone and got man-struck.

Matters didn't improve in the morning. Just as we were about to set out, a very groggy delegation from the new party—the Mills Party, as they were known—approached Miss Simpson. Hats shakily swept off revealed bleary eyes.

"Ma'am?" the leader inquired.

"Yes?" Miss Simpson was her haughty best in her disapproval. In her book, dissipations should never interfere with progress.

"Well, ma'am. Seein' as how your party did have the lead on us, we was wonderin' if you'd mind us tagging to your rear for a ways."

"If you choose to swallow our dust, it makes no difference to me."

"Thankin' you for your consideration, ma'am."

Hats were returned, and shortly the Mills Party wagons were being kicked, cajoled, and sworn into our rear. Amelia was beaming. A few wagons ahead, Lizzie O'Malley was in a similar state of euphoria. Only the Kennan twins sniffed in sympathy with Miss Simpson. Sour grapes didn't sit well on them.

Midmorning we passed by another big rock, called Devil's Gate on account of the way the Sweetwater River cut through its middle. It might have been fun to try and climb up its cliffs to peer down at the water rampaging through, but it wasn't near enough to the nooning yet, and Miss Simpson was trying to make up for time lost on the holiday. The Mills Party did stop, though, and Amelia kept casting back longing glances as we moved on ahead. She probably expected that young man, and the entire Mills Party, too, no doubt, to join up with us straight through to Oregon. She was acting as if a few dances shared under the starlight shining over Independence Rock could change everything.

By midafternoon Amelia and Lizzie O'Malley both were dispossessed of that dream. The Mills Party, fifty wagons strong, passed us with evident relish. Strive though Miss Simpson might to eat *their* dust, by evening we were on our own again. As my sister and I unyoked oxen to graze on stunted prairie marred by the Mills Party's passing, I glanced at her.

"Too bad about the grass, Amelia."

"I hope Wade Jennings's oxen choke on whatever grazing they find ahead. Who needs men anyway!"

"I've been saying that all along—"

"Shut up, Phoebe."

Three days past the last sight of the Mills Party, I was beginning to wonder why the Brown family hadn't been blessed with wealth. If we'd had enough money back at Fort Laramie, we could have filled our wagon with the fort's exorbitantly priced flour and bacon. Then again, if we'd had enough money to begin with, we'd never be on the trail to Oregon in the first place. Supplies were getting low once more, and our family wasn't the only one short on rations.

The Kennan twins and even Happy Hawkins had bagged a few more rabbits. But no matter how fat, a rabbit could only go so far—and never, seemingly, past one family's cookfire. I'd taken a few more potshots at the creatures myself, without noticeable luck. I was beginning to strongly doubt if that rifle and I would ever accomplish anything useful together.

Amelia had begun searching for rattlesnakes again, so I knew she was more than hungry. She hadn't been willing to look cross-eyed at rattlesnake stew since our powder had first been spoiled way back at the Kansas River crossing. What had happened to all that bounteous game that was supposed to be roving over these plains? Had the Mills Party shot it all first?

I was thinking these thoughts, feeling ravenous and sorry for myself. It was the afternoon we'd struggled past a boggy mire of water just sitting in pan-flat ponds, looking and smelling treacherous. Treacherous or not, the oxen wanted it. We had a hard time hauling them from danger. Mr. Harley had warned me about bad water.

"Let your beasts get their muzzles into alkaline water and it's all over, missy," he'd said, along with quite a few other pieces of advice that were still coming back to me in dribs and drabs. It had been a long day of work on that shooting range by Laramie, and Mr. Harley had enjoyed making free with his counsel to captive ears. "Your dumb ox will drink till he's full, then just stretch out on the prairie—bloated worse than any balloon—and die on you from the stomachache."

For an unlettered person from Kentucky, Mr. Harley certainly had known a whole lot.

Now our oxen were half black-and-blue from beatings they'd never understand were for their own benefit. Amelia and I were fairly sore ourselves. That's when I noticed the smoke in the air.

"Smell something, Amelia?"

She didn't even shift her gaze as we trudged on. "Only wisps from the dying embers of love lost."

Apparently Wade Jennings was still on her mind. I sniffed the air again. "That must be some powerful blaze you two kindled at the Rock, because I think your Mr. Jennings is sending smoke signals back to us."

"Don't be absurd, Phoebe." She finally scanned the horizon before us. "Goodness! Smoke! And thickening fast." Her eyes shot north and south. "Approaching in a solid sweep . . . I do believe the entire prairie is on fire!"

I squinted hard through the growing haze. "And something's coming out of it, fast."

Miss Simpson must have finally noticed, too,

because "Halt wagons!" was peremptorily bellowed down the line.

We halted, but hadn't even time to ease the oxen from their yokes. A low ocean of flames was precipitously following the smoke—and between that tide and the foglike smoke in advance of it was a rampaging line of beasts.

"Buffalo!"

"Fire!"

The cries went up simultaneously.

Lord, I prayed. *Which should I tend to first? My empty stomach or the wagon?* Here, at last, was game—but Papa was in the wagon, and certainly couldn't fend for himself. The whole contraption was dry as tinder from days without rain. Even our recent crossings back and forth over the Sweetwater River hadn't eased its complaints. That river was more like a Massachusetts creek and never did come higher than halfway up the wheels.

I prayed to God and I prayed to the Great Spirit, just for good measure. Meanwhile, I went for a water bag and began drenching the wagon. Amelia had rushed for the rifle and was feverishly loading it. Mama had the other water bag. Taking no chances, she was dousing it directly into the wagon, all over Papa and her precious cherrywood dresser.

"What in God's name are you doing, woman? Have you clean lost your mind? . . . Is that smoke I smell?"

"It is, Henry. Close your mouth and stop distracting me. You needed a bath anyway."

My water bag empty, I took the risk of studying our situation. The fire was still closing in, the buffalo almost upon us. Maybe it had been a useless gesture to waste all that water. Those pitiful squirts of moisture had hardly washed the dust off the sides of the whitetop. The fire didn't look to stop just because we were in its path, either. Oven-hot and relentless, it looked like it had been dining on the endless prairie for miles and we were about to become its dessert.

As for those buffalo, well, they were close enough now that you could begin to make out the froth on their heaving sides, and the saliva dripping from their panting mouths. The very ground was shaking beneath me from the thundering of their hooves.

The herd mentality had taken over. The buffalo would run right through us, is what they'd do. They'd stampede directly over us, leaving our bits and pieces for the fire to finish off.

That herd mentality was working on some of our women, too. But instead of running like the buffalo, they clumped together, wringing their hands and screeching.

Rendered near helpless by the sight myself, I could think of nothing better to do than lick my forefinger and hold it up to judge the wind. All day the dry, endless prairie wind had been blowing steadily east. The realization hit my finger before it moved up to my brain. It wasn't possible . . . but maybe it was.

The wind had shifted. It had shifted! In moments! Now it was blowing due north. I peered ahead. Could it be that the buffalo were slowing? *Thank you, God. Thank you, Great Spirit, too.*

Deliverance was at hand but I was still frozen in place, watching that entire herd of buffalo—scores of them—pause in mid-gallop. They lifted their mighty, shaggy heads. They sniffed. Less than fifty feet from the first wagon in our train they changed course with the wind.

The fire followed the wind too. It just sizzled dead in one direction and took on a fresh challenge, still tickling the tails of the buffalo. Our party hadn't the means of stopping that fire anyhow.

But the buffalo were a different matter.

Half the women who weren't wringing their hands and screeching had chosen to protect their wagons with water. The other half had gone for the food. Amelia, Lizzie O'Malley, and the Kennan twins; Happy Hawkins and Mrs. Davis—they were all stretched out before us in a defensive line not unsimilar to that shooting range back in Laramie. Legs staunchly set beneath brightly colored cotton skirts and petticoats, rifles shouldered, these women truly looked like Amazons—Amazons set to hold off the barbarians, or die trying.

When the herd halted to turn, our women took their first shots directly into that wall of meat on the hoof. It would have been fairly hard to miss, even for me. Those buffalo were a lot bigger than the jugs at Fort Laramie.

In record time the women reloaded and shot out again. As the buffalo herd disappeared between the furies of smoke and fire, it left a few sacrificial victims behind. Already the acrid odor of sizzling pelts assaulted my nostrils as I reached the fallen bodies spread on the broiling plains.

"How many did you get?" I called out. I was too busy stamping out leftover sparks beneath my boots to count for myself.

Amelia answered, singed but ecstatic.

"Eight. We got eight!"

THREE

*W*e pretty much had to lay over right there for a day. The prairie ahead was too dangerous, covered as it was with stray sparks and cinders from the great fiery cataclysm. There was all that meat to deal with, too.

Once everyone was truly convinced the dangers of fire and stampede were past, we stood around admiring our bounteous future meals.

"Goodness." I was nothing if not impressed. "You and Lizzie certainly did a first-rate job, Amelia!"

"Oh, pooh!" Hannah Kennan cut in. "Sarah and I bagged a few, too."

"Indeed," Sarah pointed out. "And if we hadn't the tedious necessity of reloading, sister and I could have dealt with the entire herd, single-handed."

That was too much for Happy Hawkins. "You twins are getting a mite high-handed, to my mind. I stopped at least one bull, and Mrs. Davis managed a very decent shot."

Timid, gray-haired Mrs. Davis beamed as if Happy had just bestowed a medal upon her, but the twins were loath to part with any glory. They began bickering again until I intervened.

"It doesn't matter. You *all* were fine, standing up against almost certain death the way you did." I turned. "Your father would have been real proud of you," I told the twins. I toed the nearest buffalo carcass. "And I'm past delighted. Looks as if I've finally found enough animal brains to finish the tanning job on Yellow Feather's elk-skin present. There'll be plenty enough to do up most of these other skins too."

Hannah and Sarah turned up their noses fast.

"Ugh."

"Who'd want to mess about with such mangy old leftovers?"

"*I* would."

Amelia's sudden assertion stopped me. "You would?"

She nodded a positive yes as she walked around her trophy, measuring it in her mind. Perhaps my sister had watched me fuss over my hide for too long and needed one of her own to give me a little competition. Or maybe she needed a project sufficiently monumental to distract her from thoughts of that young printer. Whatever her motives, her interest and pride were noteworthy. I would've dwelt on it longer, only Miss Simpson approached with a ravenous cast to her eyes, brandishing knives for the butchering. Amazing. Even Miss Simpson was human enough to get hungry.

"You will teach me how to do it, won't you, Phoebe? How to tan my buffalo hide?"

We were stuffing ourselves with buffalo marrow soup and buffalo steaks done to a turn that evening. In honor of the occasion we'd even released Papa from his prison for the duration of the layover. His hair was a little grayer and more grizzled in the light than I'd remembered, but otherwise he was his usual self as he sat propped up against a wagon wheel, gorging next to the rest of us.

I swallowed. "Thought it was daft to tan hides, Amelia." There was no point in wasting an opportunity to get even for former insults. "Thought it was silly and *heathen*."

"I never did call it *heathen*, Phoebe. Although I will allow that perhaps I overreacted to your earlier enthusiasm over that elk skin of yours."

"I'll say. Treating me as if I ought to be bound for bedlam or something."

"That's not so, Phoebe Brown! I only—"

"Stop your wrangling, daughters. I'm trying to digest my food."

"Yes, Papa." We both sighed.

A long moment passed.

"Well, will you?" Amelia started again. "Please?"

"Since you put it that way." I stabbed at another piece of meat. "You could have said please to begin with. What do you mean to do with your hide, anyhow?"

"It's going to be a robe for my bed in Oregon."

Mama gagged on her steak. "You'd cover yourself with that great, smelly object? In *my* new home?"

"Things are going to be different in Oregon, Mama," Amelia answered. "Remember? I suspect it will be some time before your new house attains the civilized charm of the old one in Massachusetts. And besides, the robe will be warm."

"Ought to be inspirational, too," I piped up. "For all those stories you mean to write."

"*What* stories?" thundered Papa. "*What* writing?"

Amelia sent me a glare meant to congeal every particle of food sitting in my stomach. I took pity on her. Maybe that particular cat oughtn't be let out of the bag just yet. An attractive young female with a serious mission toward literature wasn't something Papa would understand. Especially a female who also happened to be his daughter.

I bit off another monumental hunk of steak and chewed it in the sudden silence, considering my next words carefully. "Only idle talk, Papa. A person has to talk about *something* walking miles every day. Amelia and I, we've just been making up silly stories in our heads to pass the time." I turned to my sister. "You'll be needing my elk-skin frame for your buffalo robe. Let me finish treating Yellow Feather's skin tonight, and I'll hand the frame over to you tomorrow."

"Thank you, Phoebe."

Amelia's words came out with a pent-up sigh of relief. Mama glanced speculatively at the two of us. "Ladle out a little more of that soup into my bowl, Phoebe dear."

"My pleasure, Mama. How about another steak, Papa?"

Papa belched and thrust his tin bowl toward me.

It wasn't much more than fifty miles from our layover to South Pass. This was the only point in probably a thousand miles where our wagons could safely cross through the solid hump of the Rocky Mountains beginning to poke up in the distance to the north and south of us. About twenty miles from where we'd almost been destroyed by the blaze, the burned prairie suddenly returned to its unscathed condition. And sitting smack on the dividing line between scorched earth and healthy sagebrush were the remains of campfires from another party—singed black toward the east.

The prairie wind played strange tricks, indeed.

I wasn't the only one to cast accusing glares at those signs of carelessness. Miss Simpson bustled up to shove through the crowd of girls.

"Well!" she sniffed. "It would appear that the Mills Party has not amended its habits. *Arson* may now be added to its waywardness and carousing."

"I'm sure it wasn't the *entire* Mills Party responsible, Miss Simpson," Amelia tried. She was still defending her young printer. Love died hard when there wasn't anything else to think about.

"An *entire* party is responsible for each of its individuals, Amelia Brown. We all of us signed covenants to that effect before leaving Missouri."

"But there were more than fifty wagons in that train—"

"All the more eyes to sight sparks, and hands to put them out." Miss Simpson straightened from the evidence. "Let this be but another lesson to each of you, young ladies. The sloppiness"—her eyes took in the Kennan twins—"or waywardness of one may endanger the lives of all."

"Pooh and pudding!" Hannah Kennan commented as soon as Miss Simpson was out of hearing range. "If it weren't for the silly Mills people starting that fire, we'd be good and hungry this very minute. We may never have set eyes on that herd otherwise."

"Sister is right," Sarah said, adding, "Poor Daddy had to die for our first buffalo feast, and the fire brought us our next."

I shivered unaccountably and sent up a quick prayer to heaven. Surely disaster needn't be the only basis for full stomachs.

It was a mere three and a half days after we'd butchered all that meat that our wagons lumbered up a slight incline, drying strips of buffalo flapping over the whitetops' sides. There at the top was the official dividing point of the continent, the halfway mark of the trip. And just below was a well-appointed camp of tents and mules and other assorted livestock.

Next to me, Miss Prendergast squinted avidly at the view. "Just think, Phoebe. We've actually reached the place from which waters flow either to the Atlantic or the Pacific!"

I took in the sight less enthusiastically. "I thought it would be more impressive, making it to South Pass and conquering the Rockies, Miss Prendergast. This looks like just another hill, not the beginning of the official Oregon Country."

"But it is, Phoebe. It is! *All* Oregon Country from this point on." The schoolmistress in her took over as she swept a delicate arm north to south. "From Russian Alaska clear down to Spanish California! All the land in between! All the way to the Pacific Ocean! With equal rights of settlement between Americans and the British since the War of 1812."

Maybe I still didn't look impressed enough, because Miss Prendergast amended her enthusiasm a little. "Well, perhaps it is another thousand miles to Oregon City itself. But the end of our travails is almost at hand!"

I was about to point out what a sizable number of travails a thousand miles could bring. Luckily, Mama intervened.

"People!" She descended with ill-concealed groans from her hard wagon seat behind us. "Other human beings! Camped just as comfortably as you could please. Who do you suppose they are?"

Amelia joined us. "Maybe the Mills Party?" The fervor of her words proved my sister was willing to forgive all.

"Why don't we just go and find out for you, Mama?" I offered. "Then again, maybe you'd like to come along—"

"I need a dipper of water, Ruth!" Papa ordered

from the wagon. "I'm as parched as the afternoon."

Mama gave me a helpless shrug and reached for the dipper. Amelia and I, trailed by Miss Prendergast, raced to loose the oxen before taking off for the other camp.

It didn't take long to find out about those strangers. As we arrived, a handsome, sandy-haired, slim young man was already stepping up on a box, motioning for our other curious party members to gather round. In a moment his presence and purpose became clear.

"Ladies and gentlemen," he began. He stopped to really look at us. "Er . . . well, anyway, *ladies*. I stand here ready to bring you tidings of great import." With a dramatic flourish he held up a letter, cleared his throat impressively, and began reading from it: " 'At the Headwaters of the Sweetwater: To all California Emigrants now on the Road . . .' "

It took a while to figure out what all the young man was going on about, but the letter turned out to be from somebody named Lansford W. Hastings. The gist of it was that the United States was now at war with Mexico and this Hastings person was waiting up ahead at Fort Bridger to personally guide California-bound parties safely through on Hastings's new cutoff south of the Great Salt Lake.

The young man finished and gave us a dazzling smile as he carefully folded the missive. He did have a nice set of teeth. "Any questions, ladies?"

Hannah Kennan raised her hand, but Happy Hawkins swatted it down. "We ain't got any, as we ain't got any truck with Mexico, and ain't making for California anyhow. Would like to know what your Mr. Hastings stands to gain out of all this, though."

"Madam." The dazzling expression turned pained. "Madam. My partner, Mr. Hastings, will gain nothing from this venture—aside from the usual guide fee of ten dollars per wagon. His motives are purely humanitarian—"

"Ten dollars per!" huffed Happy. "That don't sound too humanitarian to me!"

"Now, madam," the young man rejoined. "Mr. Hastings merely desires that all know of the bountiful opportunities present in California. Why, on that golden shore men neither strive nor strain. Fruits of the earth and vines practically fall into their outstretched hands—"

"Do they fall into women's hands as well?" Miss Prendergast sweetly inquired. She peered more closely at Hastings's agent through her wire-framed glasses. "And correct me if I should be wrong, but does not California belong to Spanish Mexico? And should not the mankind of Mexico already be engaged in picking up all that fresh fruit?"

"Madam, madam—"

"It's *Miss*, thank you."

"Miss—"

"Enough nonsense!" boomed Miss Simpson. "We're not now, nor ever have been, bound for California. We'll work for our fruits in Oregon. You may seek others, less wary, to ply your tricks upon, young man. Miss Simpson's party shall not be hornswoggled." She turned. "Come along, ladies. There's camp to set up."

"But . . . but . . ."

We left the speaker stuttering to himself. Walking back to our wagons, Hannah complained about not being allowed to speak. Lizzie O'Malley shut her up fast.

"And what was it you were wanting to ask, Hannah Kennan? The color of the young man's eyes? Blue they were, like the ocean. Not a drop of Indian blood in that one."

Hannah mumbled something that sounded like *fiddlesticks,* and she and Sarah turned for their own wagon.

Back at our whitetop Mama already had the

supper fire going. "What was all that about, girls?"

"Not the Mills Party," mourned Amelia.

"Nothing much, Mama," I added. "Just somebody trying to talk us into taking the desert route to California instead of carrying on to Oregon."

"No new women to speak with, then?" The sigh that followed my "nope" was philosophical. "You may as well see to your father. Maybe he needs more water."

"Yes, Mama." I banged on the side of the wagon. "How you doing in there, Papa? And why would we be at war with Mexico?" That had been bothering me. "What have the Mexicans ever done to us?"

"We're at war with *Mexico*?" That gave him something new to think about. "Nothing, daughter. They've done nothing. . . . It's more like the other way around, if you consider their poor luck in losing Texas to us, and their justifiable lack of enthusiasm over having the same happen with California."

"Can we do that? Just take over somebody's land that way?"

"What in thunder you think we're heading out to Oregon for, Phoebe? The British could be a mite upset about that, too." Papa stopped. "Then again, it might all be settled before we arrive."

"Settled between whom?"

"Between Washington and London, on where the final borders for the Northwest Territories—the Oregon Country—will lie."

"Oh."

First Miss Prendergast with her War of 1812 and now Papa. Today was the first I'd heard about the British having a hand in Oregon. And here I'd thought all this Oregon Country sort of belonged to the Indians, and they were maybe going to share a little of it with us Americans—there being so much of it around.

It wasn't that I was dull-witted. I already knew well enough that the Pawnee and the Sioux had no desire to share anything. I couldn't blame them for that. . . . Where had I gotten the idea that other tribes of Indians farther west might think differently? I helped myself to a long drink of water before passing the dipper to my father. Papa might have a few failings, but I'd never considered him dishonest. He must know more than he was explaining to me. He must have begun this journey in good faith, going after legal land.

The remainder of the evening was quiet except for the late arrival of a train that we never even knew had been behind us. They called themselves the Donner Party, but that was all we learned about them, because as we were starting off again the next morning they were laying over to listen to the Lansford Hastings sales pitch.

We took the Dry Sandy down to the Big Sandy, then trudged through a parched patch of land till we caught up with another creek called Blacks Fork. That was just before Fort Bridger.

It's lucky none of us had wasted any thought on grand notions about Fort Bridger, like we had before Fort Laramie. It had greener surroundings, true, set as it was on rich bottomland kept moist by waters streaming down from the nearby Bear River Mountains. But Fort Bridger itself had even less to brag about. There were a couple of dilapidated log cabins, but no sign of Jim Bridger, the famous old mountain man who owned the place. Wasn't any sign of that Lansford Hastings supposedly lying in wait for his California victims, either, only a few loutish gamblers we could see from a distance.

Miss Simpson settled the party on some decent grass nearby and forbade any of us girls to go near the stockade. It seemed a pity, since we had learned quite a bit from men almost as bedraggled back at Laramie. Mr. Harley came immediately to my mind, not that I'd caught my rabbit stew yet, nor felt anywhere nearer to doing so. But Miss Simpson was definite. And that was it for Fort Bridger.

Maybe some of those men would have told us about Soda Springs, because they were a surprise when we came upon them a hundred-odd miles farther along the trail. They might have warned us about the Snakes, too—the river and Indians both—given half a chance. But perhaps being unprepared was better.

FOUR

*F*irst off, after leaving Fort Bridger, the buffalo chips disappeared. There wasn't a blessed one to be found as the plains changed into low, barren hills. Funny how you can miss something you've spent so much time grumbling over. Now, instead of a bushel or two of chips to make a good evening fire, we were reduced to yanking out sagebrush by its shallow roots, or tying together bunches of dry grass to keep the supper fires going. Mama skimmed ash from the dinner pot one evening and glanced at Amelia and me ruefully.

"Those chips were so much neater to use. Almost like proper charcoal. I suppose that's the end of the buffalo, too."

"What?" Somehow I'd never made the connection. "No more herds to hunt? I didn't even get in a shot!"

Amelia, who was still working on her furry robe, smiled superiorly. "As if you'd actually hit anything. Would you prefer turning back to the plains for another chance to catch up with the Kennans' record, Phoebe?"

"Never!" I ignored Amelia's jibe, even if it was sadly true. "But I did so want a chance to gallop old Blackie into a big herd, take aim, and—"

"And get gored like Mr. O'Malley, I suppose?" Amelia taunted.

"Or have your legs splintered like mine!" snapped Papa from the wagon.

"No! I just wanted to *try* to shoot as well as those blasted Kennan twins, is all."

"Phoebe! Your tongue!"

"Well, nearly as well, Mama. Always showing off the way they are, taking potshots at anything that moves the livelong day—"

"And wasting useful gunpowder, daughter," Papa countered through his thin wall of canvas.

"Well, if there aren't any more buffalo, or elk, or even jackrabbits to be had, what is there left to hunt? And I don't mean hawks and such like. It seems a crime to be shooting at things that fly through the sky."

"And so it is, daughter," Mama soothed. "I can't imagine where Tabitha Kennan's mind is to allow her daughters such errant ways. There's a certain freedom to the birds of the air . . . soaring as they do while we must plod. They make a kind of connection between this earth and the heavens. . . ." She plaintively shoved another bunch of sagebrush under the pot and waved away the new flurry of ash.

"Never fear, little sister," Amelia said. "We'll be in proper mountains soon. There ought to be deer or antelope. Maybe even bear."

That cheered me up. "Bear! Say, now that would be something to hunt! More impressive than buffalo even—and what a robe a bear skin would make! Why, I could even use pieces of one to trim that dress I hope to make from Yellow Feather's elk skin—"

"Ah, yes. The once and future Sioux dress."

I turned on my sister. "Just because I've been taking my time, admiring my finished skin, doesn't mean I won't get around to it, Amelia."

"Used to be bears in Massachusetts, Phoebe. In my youth," Papa broke in again. Probably to end what he judged as a potential wrangle. "Even small, eastern bears are a fair handful. Can't say I'd care to come up against one of those western grizzlies I've heard about."

I made a face at Amelia before acknowledging Papa's conversational attempts. He was trying to be pleasant. Trying to make believe he wasn't still stuck inside the wagon, with us at liberty out here. Maybe his legs were feeling better today. "Where'd you hear about them, Papa? You haven't talked to anyone but us in months."

Papa's snort came forth clearly. "In my days of freedom, daughter. Before I was in thrall to this miserable wagon. Before I had to make conversation with a homicidal cherrywood dresser . . . Years back in Independence, Missouri."

A stray breeze sparked up the sagebrush under the cookpot just then, and Amelia and I were too busy swatting out the flames that caught onto Mama's skirt hem to pursue the subject of bears any further.

But we'd hooked up with the Bear River by then, and even though there were no creatures of that persuasion in evidence, the hope stayed with me. I took to lugging the family rifle during part of our daily walks next to the oxen. Amelia finally noticed.

"Surely you don't expect a bear to just walk up to us on the trail? Or even hop past like a rabbit!"

"Even if I did, Amelia, it wouldn't matter. The rifle's not loaded."

"Then why, in heaven's name, are you bothering to carry it?"

"Well, for starters, I wanted to look as efficient as Hannah and Sarah. But on second thought, I didn't want to shoot off my foot by accident. Mr. Harley was very particular about how to handle a loaded gun, if you'll remember."

Amelia shook her head. "I don't think I'll ever fully understand how your mind works, Phoebe. Thank goodness mine functions in a more logical progression. And why you'd even consider trying to emulate those two flighty twins—"

"They haven't been all that flighty recently, Amelia. Not without any eligible Indian braves around—" I stopped as raucous shrieks sped down the line of wagons. "Maybe I spoke too soon. The Kennans are leading the train today, aren't they, Amelia?"

"Yes. And that sounded like their dulcet tones." She sped past her oxen's side toward the head of the line before I had a chance to do it first. I muttered protests, but had to remain with the beasts nevertheless.

The Kennans had topped another bald hill with their lead wagon and stopped short at the sight spread below. When I finally halted our oxen and got up front to see, I knew why. In the flats between our hill and the next was an eroded, pockmarked landscape spouting and spewing and steaming into the dry blue sky.

"Well, that certainly took a long time," I remarked to no one in particular.

Margaret O'Malley huffed up next to me. "What took a long time?" She grasped the view. "Merciful saints!"

"Back at my Young Ladies' Seminary in Massachusetts, one of my teachers said as how anything past Independence, Missouri, was a 'lunar landscape.' It just took us over eleven hundred miles to find that moon, is all."

Margaret's freckled nose was wrinkled. "You think the moon smells this bad? Da insists it's made of green cheese—his favorite—but this smells more like rotten eggs."

Miss Prendergast had joined us by this time. "How delightful! Mineral waters! Possibly even a small geyser. It must be that Soda Springs my guidebook mentioned."

"Soda Springs?" Tarnation. I'd been ignoring Miss Prendergast and Mr. Judd and our evening chats over her guidebook for too long. What other surprises lay ahead that Miss Prendergast already anticipated? More moonscapes?

Suddenly a spout of water burst about three feet into the air, right in front of us. Even I gasped. Miss Prendergast happily chattered on.

"Only consider the therapeutic benefits to our

invalids if we bathe them in those waters!" She paused to wipe at the unexpected moisture on her glasses with a dainty, lace-edged handkerchief. "I must go and convince Miss Simpson to stop early for the evening."

As Miss Prendergast dashed off full of hope, Margaret made a face. "Imagine making such a spectacle of herself. A spinster of her age—at least thirty, Ma says. She'd do practically anything for that Mr. Judd, wouldn't she?"

"You noticed."

"And how could I not? Da won't be any too pleased at the stopping place, either. Even without a gored stomach he hated his monthly baths. It was the only way Ma could ever get him to change his long underwear, though. She'll have to be peeling it off him this time, after all those months in our wagon."

The thought of peeling beefy, mustachioed Mr. O'Malley might have made me sick right there on the spot if I hadn't heard Miss Simpson roar out the orders for our halt. Miss Prendergast had won this round for her blacksmith. Which meant that Amelia and Mama and I were probably going to have to lug Papa into one of those steaming pits below, too.

Of our four male invalids, only Happy Hawkins's daft husband truly enjoyed those therapeutic waters. Though they didn't seem to do his vacant mind any particular good, he splashed away happily with little Timothy, Mary Rose, and Maureen O'Malley. Zachary Judd soaked stoically in hot sulphur waters up to his chin. Papa and Mr. O'Malley sat fuming in separate facing pools, only their long red underwear peeping through the dark waters. You'd think they'd at least have been content to visit with each other after all this time, but all they did was complain.

Amelia and Mama and I grew weary of listening and wandered off to experiment with some of the hotter pools. It was Mama's idea.

"Why need we fuss with cookfires and sagebrush ashes this evening, daughters? If we were to boil buffalo jerky in this water . . . even brew a pot of coffee . . ."

The food and drink did taste a little different, but not as horrible as Papa made out, eating in his pool. He pounded his empty coffee cup onto a calcified ledge within reach. "And when is this regimen of terror to be completed?"

"By bedtime, I should think, Henry."

"Another hour or more?" Papa roared.

"Hush, Henry. Think of the fortunes the

wealthy in Europe spend to take the waters at fancy spas. Consider yourself fortunate the Lord has blessed this great country with similar amenities, free for any passing soul. You always did think of yourself as a Democrat."

Mama's foray into politics was too much for me. I was satisfied that the springs had saved me cleaning the dishes and kettle with dry sand after the meal. I went off in search of the other girls. We splashed around in one of the pools ourselves—in only our flannel vests and petticoats—until it began growing dark. The water was fizzy and tickled all over. It also tasted incredibly putrid, as I discovered when Margaret playfully shoved my head under.

"Not fair!" I came up spitting and gagging. Margaret found that funny.

"Such a face, Phoebe Brown! If you could only see!"

It was time for revenge.

"I shall!"

I dunked Margaret, and her face *did* give me a mirror image of my own. That got us to laughing so hard we hardly had the energy to attack our big sisters. But somehow we found the strength.

Rejuvenated by all those minerals, the O'Malleys and Amelia and I wrung out our petticoats and slipped our dresses back over our heads. Then we worked out a cooperative system of hoisting our fathers from their pools and back into their wagons.

"We should have thought of this sooner," I puffed as we dispensed with Mr. O'Malley at last.

Margaret crawled out of her family wagon, wiping damp hands on her skirt. "There now. That's that. All pink and shiny and clean, our Da is."

Mrs. O'Malley poked her head into the white-top to observe the results. "And wrinkled as a new-born babe! Underwear and all. Isn't he sweet?"

"Shut your gobs, women!" Gerald O'Malley roared. "Or I'll get my revenge on reaching Oregon!"

"And how do you propose to do that, husband?"

"I'll . . . I'll . . . I'll not be taking a bath for a full year!"

"Then you'd best be readying yourself to sleep with the cow, Gerald."

Mrs. O'Malley brayed at her own humor, and Lizzie blushed. Margaret only turned to me. "And don't you think Ma doesn't mean it, Phoebe. She's getting that full of herself lately since Da didn't die on her as she expected back at Laramie."

"Our papa takes a bath every Saturday night. When we're in a civilized house—"

Amelia pulled at my arm. "Come along, Phoebe. Some family habits should remain private."

"But if Papa didn't bathe for a full year, surely everyone would know it—"

"Phoebe!"

"All right, Amelia. You needn't pinch that way. I'm coming."

When we finally met up with the Snake River, we also found Fort Hall. It was a Hudson's Bay Company trading post all stockaded against the Snake Indians. I suppose we might have taken time to be impressed by the neatness and the organization and the British accents of the place after Forts Bridger and Laramie, but what ended up getting our attention was those Snake Indians.

We'd barely made a quick exploration inside and settled our wagons on the flat plain outside the fort's walls when a contingent of Snakes approached, wanting to trade. They bore glorious fish. They also bore strings of other objects which on closer inspection turned even Happy Hawkins slightly green. Not believing my eyes, I edged closer to one of the bearers.

"What in the world—"

A vast salmon was waved before me. I'd seen the Atlantic Ocean version once or twice back in Massachusetts.

"Fish swim upriver now. Lay eggs. I catch." The

Indian showing off his wares was young, not much older than myself. Like the others, he wore his hair long and flowing down his back, the same as mine. His sun-darkened chest was bare save for loops of some kind of shell beads. It wasn't the fish or the necklace that interested me, though. It was that other string of objects slung over his back. I pointed.

"What are they?"

He smiled shyly. "Big chief in fort, he calls this 'dessert.' Maybe you like too?"

"Phoebe!" It was my big sister. "Do get away from those horrors!"

But the Indian boy had already set down his fish and was waving his dessert before my eyes.

I gulped. "Lizards. And grasshoppers. And, and *grubs*! You eat these?"

He turned to check on his elders, who were negotiating with the older women. I looked around too. My sister had deserted me. And the twins were preoccupied. Tabitha Kennan hadn't managed to incarcerate her daughters fast enough. They were eyeing two Snake braves with undiluted interest. Those young men had dropped their own salmon and were in the process of reaching out to touch the golden hair before them.

"Very good roasted."

I spun back to the Snake boy. Hannah and

Sarah got admiration. I got a lecture on edible insects. "I don't believe you."

He pulled a half-charred grub from the end of the string and popped it into his mouth, chewing with evident pleasure. Then he pulled off another one and offered it to me. "I make gift. Eat."

I had survived Indian dog back at Scotts Bluff, but somehow a *grub* . . .

"White people scared," he taunted slyly. "White girls most."

"That isn't so!" I snatched the thing from his out-stretched hand and popped it into my own mouth. It lay there a moment, exuding a smoky flavor. Steeling myself, I bit down. The thing crunched. I could feel that crunch clear down my spine to my toes. I crunched again and swallowed. It hadn't been that bad at all. Sort of nutty, like a burned chestnut. I grinned. Let Hannah and Sarah top that one. "See?"

He reached for his string again, pointing at a grasshopper.

"Why not?"

The wings and legs were a little hard to handle, but I stomached them, too.

The boy suddenly laughed. "Maybe wrong about white people. You want to buy? Trade for beads or gunpowder."

"I'm sorry, but my mother must do the trading."

"Where father? Where men?"

It was all too obvious that our men weren't around to protect us. Fortunately, the fort was. I felt I could be candid for once. "Our men are mostly dead or hurt. Big accident many months—moons—past."

"Ac-ci-dent?"

"Um. Mistake. Big trouble. With buffalo."

He nodded wisely. "No buffalo here. Know stories. Make thunder over land."

"They certainly do."

He lowered his creatures to the ground gently and pointed to his chest. "Me Red Fish. Like flesh of great *sammon*."

"No!" I couldn't believe it. I pointed to my own chest. "Me Swift Fish. Blood sister to Sioux." I held out the scar on my right palm. He inspected it gravely.

"Great honor." He glanced at the nearby crowd of women who were apparently completing negotiations. "Them too?"

"Only me." I couldn't help being proud of that fact. He noticed.

"You catch fish? . . . Hunt?" He held his arms outstretched, as if he were holding a rifle.

"I swim. And I can shoot."

"Other women . . . squaws. Shoot too?"

"Yes. Shoot good. As good as any Indian."

"Hah!" He picked up his trading items. "We see."

"See what?"

But Red Fish was trotting off after his half-dozen elders, chattering very fast in his language, motioning back toward me. There was a round of disbelieving laughter followed by more interested, considering stares in my direction, then in that of the older women. Somehow I wasn't convinced all that interest was to the benefit of Miss Simpson's Petticoat Party.

We were just finishing an early supper of rich salmon roasted over the fire. It was delicious, but I was still a little worried about those Snakes. They weren't exactly Sioux, whom I could trust. It was only a slight uneasiness, a niggling sensation about my conversation with Red Fish and what he might have said to the other Indians. About our traveling without the protection of able-bodied men. About how that could be interpreted by the Snakes as an open invitation to take advantage of our train. We could be plundered—or worse. . . . Not that I'd mentioned the talk to any of the others—especially not my family. Then again, come morning we'd be safely gone, journeying farther and farther along the river from this particular band of Indians. Yes, it would happen that way.

"Mama, Phoebe. Look." It was Amelia. "Those Indians are coming back. Without their fish."

I tried to make myself smaller. Amelia noticed.

"And they're heading straight this way. What have you been up to, Phoebe?"

"Why, Amelia, what could Phoebe possibly have to do with—"

The Snakes surrounded our family fire. Miss Simpson and Happy Hawkins scurried to their rear. Before I could even rise, one of the Indians spoke. The one called Red Fish was smirking behind.

"Blood sister make challenge. We accept. At first light in morning. By fishing grounds."

Miss Simpson had finally barreled through the crowd. "To what are you referring? What challenge?"

The Snake brave recognized Miss Simpson. "You too. All squaws. Bring guns. We fix test." Nodding with authority to the others, the Snake leader and his followers decorously left our camp without another glance. Miss Simpson, unfortunately, was still with us.

"Phoebe Brown! What mischief have you been into now?"

"Ruth!" Papa bawled from the wagon. "What in tarnation's happening out there?"

My head swung from the wagon to my mother to Miss Simpson. "I think the Snakes have just now challenged us to a shooting match."

FIVE

I didn't get much sleep that night. First there was Miss Simpson and my family swarming all over me. Next, and worse, came the girls. Hannah and Sarah Kennan were the only ones delighted by the turn of events. Delirious would be closer to the mark.

"What fun! Finally we'll be able to demonstrate our talents, sister. For all the world to see!"

"Indeed, Hannah. All our efforts, all our work to become superior marksmen will not have been in vain."

"Surely not." Hannah paused. "I'm not positive that I want to beat a certain one of those young braves, though, Sarah."

"The one with the fish-teeth bracelet? But that would be cheating, sister dear."

"In a good cause, I'm positive, Sarah. Did you see how his muscles rippled behind all that salmon? And yet . . . Gracious, but isn't life just filled with temptations—"

"And all of them fascinating!"

Hannah and Sarah eventually waltzed off to oil their rifles. I merely swatted at mosquitoes while sitting by our fire till it burned down to nothing. As yet I hadn't managed to hit a single moving creature with the family rifle. How could I have boasted so blithely to Red Fish? Stuffed as it was, my stomach felt hollow.

"That's another thing about buffalo chips, Amelia," I commented inconsequentially to the figure huddled inside the blankets next to me. "They surely did chase off mosquitoes."

Amelia only twitched. Eventually I slid into my own blankets.

First light found most of our train shivering in the coolness down by the Snake River, just outside Fort Hall's walls. Miss Simpson's Party was standing to one side, the waiting Indians in a quiet group to the other. Discreetly in the distance was a cluster of squaws, small children peeking curiously from behind their mothers' buckskin skirts.

There was yet another throng assembling, as well. Somehow the men from the fort had got wind of the event. They were slowly trickling out from the shelter of the stockade, half asleep, yet intent on a little rare entertainment. They stood around in clumps, measuring up us girls like we were meat on the hoof. Amelia and Lizzie O'Malley were about to take offense when we all caught on to the conversation. Far from assessing our finer aspects, those mountain men were making bets on us! Gambling!

Giving vent to the anger rising within me, I stomped over to the nearest hunter. "Now look here, you! You've no right to treat us as if we were a card game!"

He threw back his head and laughed. "I think the lass wants a piece of our winnings!" His companions roared and slapped their thighs. One fetched out a hip flask and took a swig. They were waking up fast.

"Well, then." Another wiped tears from his eyes. "She'll just have to see that her aim is off, won't she. Not that there'll be any danger of these puny females beating Novoka and his men."

Puny females? "We'll see about that! Obviously you haven't heard about the Petticoat Party!"

I stalked back to my own group, furious. "It's even worse than we thought. Those trappers are betting *against* us!"

Amelia's eyes became hard. "Calm yourself, Phoebe. You'll upset your shooting arm." She turned to the Kennan twins. "And no nonsense from you two, either. We're shooting fair and straight. This is a matter of honor for our sex."

The twins may have been set to protest, but at that moment a breeze blew the last of the river's mists away. The sun seemed suddenly to rise. And the leader of the Snakes—Novoka himself—stepped forth into the clearing between us.

"White squaws without men," he began. "*You* ask for challenge. *We* set terms."

That wasn't exactly fair. I'd never asked for a challenge. Since when did a little boasting make a challenge? I looked at Novoka and sighed. Probably since now. Indians didn't seem to think precisely the same way we did.

Novoka continued. "All shoot, in turn. Squaws win, Novoka and his people give much smoked *sammon*. Novoka and his people win"—the chief paused and almost smiled—"squaws give six guns and one horse. Red Fish choose horse."

My eyes searched the crowd of Snakes and found Red Fish grinning to beat the band. That sneaky, trickerous grub. He needed a horse of his own, no doubt about it. And his own rifle, too. The other guns would be gravy. Those Snakes might not think exactly the same as us, but the end result was pretty much the same.

Novoka was looking to Miss Simpson for confirmation of the terms. Miss Simpson herself turned only long enough to catch my eye. I could read what she was thinking, clear as day. "Phoebe Brown," she was saying. "Phoebe Brown, *you* and you alone are responsible for this folly. Lose the match and *you* will pay." She swiveled back to the chief. "Your terms are clear. They are far from acceptable, but will be honored."

Novoka nodded and made a motion for us to follow him as he led us along the riverbank. He stopped where a shooting range had been prepared. I stared, amazed.

Fish heads.

They'd set salmon heads on stakes tightly pounded into the ground at intervals. There were four rows of twelve targets each. The first three rows were just bony skeleton heads. The fourth row was made up of fresh heads, vacant eyes staring back at us. I squinted at those eyes. I had to, they were so far off.

"Six." Novoka held up six fingers. "Six only will shoot, each side."

I heaved a sigh of relief. That had to leave me out. No way was I one of our best marksmen. Novoka's next words deprived me of that relief.

"Swift Fish"—he pointed to me—"must be one."

"So it's back to *Swift Fish,* is it?" Miss Simpson's

words were so sharp, they practically cut. "Do let us learn, then, Miss Phoebe *Swift Fish* Brown, how well you can swim through *this* river."

She stopped to consider the rest of our train. "Hannah and Sarah Kennan, front and center. Also Amelia Brown and Lizzie O'Malley. Happy Hawkins—" She regarded her right-hand woman. "I'm counting on you, Happy. Don't let me down."

We, the chosen, walked forth with our weapons. Amelia had the family rifle that we'd have to share. The Snakes came forward to shoot first. I looked for Red Fish, but apparently Novoka was taking no chances with youngsters. His competitors included three older men, and three strapping young braves—including, naturally, the two who had been admiring the twins' golden locks.

One by one the Snakes demonstrated their prowess. Standing on a line etched into the hard ground, they casually demolished the first six targets, then moved off stolidly, no expression on their faces.

It was our turn.

Hannah and Sarah went first. They easily wiped out their allotted targets. So did Amelia, Lizzie, and Happy. Now it was my chance. Amelia handed me the reloaded rifle. "I'm not blaming you for all this, Phoebe, but *please* try your best."

I gulped, took the rifle, and spread my legs squarely beneath my skirts at the edge of the dividing line on the ground. Next, I raised the gun and squinted down the barrel at the last target on the first row. Mr. Harley's face flashed before me. I hadn't managed to get his rabbit, but, by heaven, I'd demolish this fish head for him. It wasn't going anywhere staked down that way, was it? And it wasn't any farther off than that whiskey jug at Laramie, either. My finger tightened on the trigger. The rifle didn't feel as heavy as it used to. Mentally thanking Mr. Harley for his exercises, I pulled.

"Bull's-eye!"

"She hit it!"

"Good job, daughter!"

It was Mama's voice that made me finally inspect my handiwork. I had done it. I really had. The cramping in my stomach eased up a little. Only three more shots to go.

The second round went smooth as butter. The third too. No one on either team made a single error. I was breathing more easily. Maybe I wasn't totally useless with firearms—at least, when the target couldn't possibly move. The growing chorus of enthusiasm from all our women behind didn't hurt, either. Mrs. Davis and the rest of the older widows seemed to be enjoying themselves enormously. Only pregnant Mabel Hatch seemed a trifle concerned. She was biting on her fingernails as if she hadn't had breakfast. Maybe she was still hungry. Margaret O'Malley had mentioned that women in her condition never seemed to be full.

I stood back to watch the braves line up for the final test. Sweat was sliding down my face, even though it wasn't anywhere near to hot yet. Miss Prendergast dashed up to loan me one of her lace-edged handkerchiefs.

"Phoebe, dear, I'm so proud of you! I always wanted to be a woman of action, but with these weak eyes of mine—"

"You, Miss Prendergast?" I stared at her in surprise as I swabbed at my temples. "Why, you can do so many other things!"

"But never hold up our party's honor in a shooting match, Phoebe. I can't even *see* that last row of targets."

"Thank you, Miss Prendergast. I truly hope your faith in me will be rewarded."

The final round began. The Snakes had been very silent until now, but a sudden chant rose from their crowd. Like a war cry, it was. I shivered. Their first man took his shot. Huzzahs rose up. It was good. . . . So was the second and third, all through the fifth. The sixth and last Indian approached—

Hannah's current favorite, the one with the fish-teeth bracelet. He sauntered to his spot, all arrogance. He was that sure of himself. So sure of himself that he allowed his eyes to fall upon Hannah's glowing countenance for a split second. Turning, he aimed and fired. And missed.

I spun toward Hannah. Her face plainly showed her true feelings. Aghast. Unsure. "Hannah," I whispered. "Hannah. You've got to stand up for us!"

Amelia took over. "It's our honor, Hannah. And our rifles. We don't have extras to be giving to these Snakes."

Hannah turned to her sister in supplication.

"Well, Hannah," Sarah ventured, "I'm quite certain there are yet more Indians down the trail."

That thought hit its mark far better than any of our pleas.

Hannah brightened. "You may be right, sister. There hasn't been a dearth thus far."

She squared her shoulders and marched forward. Barely sighting her target, she pierced it neatly through the one staring eye. The Snakes gasped, then let out a cheer of appreciation. Sarah followed suit after her twin. Lizzie and Amelia and Happy continued to uphold our honor.

Then it was my turn again. The last shot.

I strode toward my fate as steadfastly as I was

able. Fate? Impending doom was more like it. Truth to tell, below the grinding stomach my knees were beginning to buckle rather badly. Flukes, that's what my other good shots had been. Three in a row. I couldn't possibly keep up that record. Couldn't possibly keep up the fiction that I was an expert at this business like I'd let on to Red Fish. If I missed, I tried to reason, all would not be lost. The teams would be tied. . . . But then Novoka would probably devise some other, far harder test. And I truly wanted all this to be over and done.

With clammy hands, I raised the rifle a final time. The lone fish eye stared at me. I blinked, and it seemed to blink back. Not good. My heart was beating clear up through my ears. My arm was tiring.

Lord, I prayed. *Lord, never will I be so prideful again. If only I can make this shot. It's not as if it's a leaping rabbit. And it doesn't have to be a showy shot like Hannah's, either. Just one last, clean shot, Lord. Please.*

Murmurs were rising behind me. I dropped the rifle barrel for a long moment to wipe each hand in turn on my skirt. Taking a deep, steadying breath, I raised the barrel again. That fishy eye was still glaring directly at me, but it had stopped blinking. Well, a swift fish ought to be able to get the better of a dead one. I pulled the trigger.

A gasp went up behind me.

Had I missed? I squinted through the distance. *Thank you, Lord!*

I pivoted around. Mama was standing right behind me, beaming proudly. Miss Prendergast was dabbing at her eyes with yet another handkerchief. Miss Simpson just looked plain relieved. I let out a whoop.

"We did it!"

Those Indians turned out to be pretty good sports about it all. They brought us great slabs of smoked salmon. After it began piling up it had me worried we might be taking all their winter food. Mama was of the same opinion.

"Thank you kindly," she said, when Novoka formally approached with another armful of fish. "But it is enough. We have gifts for you, too." She turned to the small barrel of trade beads Amelia and I had lugged out of the wagon over Papa's protests. "Please. Take some."

Novoka's eyes lit up at all the gleaming red and blue and white glass baubles. At first I thought sure he was going to go for the entire barrel's worth. Instead, he called out something behind him, and Red Fish appeared, holding a handmade pouch. Red Fish didn't seem to want to catch my eye, so I poked him gently.

"Your 'dessert' was real good, Red Fish. And your *sammon* even better."

His eyes finally locked on mine. "You spoke truth, not boast. White girls *can* shoot! Red Fish believe next time." He bent to fill the pouch.

We finally hauled our wagons out of sight of Fort Hall and the Snake Indians. We hadn't heard anything more from those gambling trappers, either. They'd all lost their bets. There was only one man smiling and waving farewell to us. That was the Proctor—the head man of Fort Hall—all proper in a frock coat and white shirt and neck scarf in the middle of this wilderness. It seems he alone had backed us females.

SIX

*A*ll that prize salmon certainly did improve our morale for the next few weeks. Just thinking on how we had actually bested an entire tribe of Indians at their own game made it worthwhile getting up in the morning for another day's trek. Every time Miss Prendergast saw me she'd smile and say the same thing.

"You see, Phoebe. Miss Simpson always avowed that if we pulled together, we women could do anything!"

Not that either Miss Prendergast or Miss Simpson had been responsible for the marksmanship at the Snake shooting contest. But I wasn't about to argue the point. It was enough that the entire train was more cheerful. Papa didn't even complain about the stacks of smoked salmon competing with the cherrywood dresser for his space in the wagon.

On top of all that salmon, we had trees back again! A few trees, at any rate. There were cottonwood and willows every so often near the broad river's edge, although I fear we may have stunted their growth somewhat with our enthusiasm at finding real firewood again.

It was pretty along the Snake River, too, with the sights changing so quickly. One day it would be low mountains and cottonwood, while another day brought bare basalt cliffs with nothing but eagles and hawks and falcons soaring over them.

Those birds could fly in safety at last. The twins had stopped taking potshots at them. Not that it wasn't still a constant temptation. I caught Hannah and Sarah more than once with rifles poised and aimed, tracking the graceful creatures.

"You're not truly going after that eagle, are you, Hannah?"

"*Boom,*" Hannah whispered to herself, then lowered the barrel. "Pooh, Phoebe. Sarah and I proved ourselves sufficiently at the Snake contest."

"I guess you did come through in the end, after all."

"It's decent of you to acknowledge the fact at last, Phoebe," Sarah sniffed.

But it was true, and I wasn't the only one relieved. Amelia and Lizzie had been treating them more like equals ever since. Margaret and I, well, we privately thought the Kennans would break out in Indian fever again at the soonest opportunity.

And since we still figured that any kind of romance was more silly than not, we mainly ignored them.

Our wagons passed American Falls, where the Snake River—usually a good eight hundred feet wide—was squeezed down to a quarter of its size by great jutting hunks of rock. The rushing water fell in ten-foot steps for a fair ways. It was wonderful to see. More remarkable was that you could hear those roaring waters nearly half a day's walk beforetimes.

After listening to that water sound for hours over the creaks of our wagons, we just had to stop by the falls for our nooning. Cold salmon slabs went down fine next to the refreshing spray, but we hadn't taken into account the excitement the spectacle would cause in the younger O'Malleys. Amelia and I had to spend the remainder of rest time helping Lizzie and Margaret herd the little ones from the waterfall's edge. Young Master Timothy was nothing if not fearless, and since he'd already been saved from drowning once way back at the Platte River, he worked on the assumption that no waters could ever harm him.

"Bullheaded, just like our Da," Margaret complained as she grabbed her little brother's body from the edge yet again. "Timothy O'Malley, if you intend to ever grow as big as Da, you'll not be tempting those waters!"

"And why not, our Margaret?" asked Timothy. "Haven't I got angels watching over me like Ma says every night?"

"Don't be daft, Timothy. Ma's *praying* for those angels. In fear and trembling. You've never seen one, have you?"

He nodded yes promptly.

"Oh-ho. And what did they look like, then?"

With a great grin of mischief that wrinkled all his freckles, Timothy pointed at Margaret and me, then scampered back to the brink of danger. Margaret paused a moment too long digesting that one. I had to make a leap after the boy next. We all breathed easier after leaving that particular scenic wonder.

Then it was more sagebrush and dry grass all the way alongside the Snake River to Caldron Linn. That was just what it sounded like, once we knew what *linn* meant. It was Mrs. O'Malley who explained, on boulders next to the swirling waters of the caldron part as she hung on to her squirming son for dear life.

"Why, it's nothing but the Gaelic for waterfall, children."

"What would Gaelic be, Mrs. O'Malley?" I inquired.

"It's the old Irish tongue, Phoebe. My parents spoke it, and I too, in my youth."

"Did you have to give it up when you came to America?"

She laughed. "No more than all the Indians we've come upon have given up their tongues. Mr. O'Malley has the gift, too, but it takes English to survive in this new world, more's the pity."

I stared down into the churning waters below us. Most of the Indians we'd met thus far had spoken at least a little English. But it was the sounds of their native tongues as I'd been hearing them that I remembered. They were wild and free sounds, just like the Snake River was now making. It would be a pity if all that disappeared, the same as Mrs. O'Malley's Gaelic.

There was more white water yet to come along the next three hundred miles of the Snake: Shoshone Falls and Thousand Springs—where underground streams burst out from beneath the rimrock of the north side of the Snake, tumbling in a long row into the river—and Salmon Falls. Yet it was the Blue Mountains beyond that I could never forget. And it all became connected somehow with my birthday.

It wasn't as if our family celebrated birthdays particularly. Mama might give us an extra kiss on our rising in the morning and take on a faraway look in her eyes. She might even comment that

Amelia's birthing had been particularly easy, while mine had been particularly difficult. Then she'd share another hug and add that she'd not regretted the pain for a single moment.

But we never received a gift or remembrance, the way we did at Christmas. Anyway, after all those years of being reminded—however lovingly—of the difficulty of my coming into the world, it began to occur to me that it ought to be *Mama* receiving a gift and thanks.

My thirteenth birthday was different.

But I'm getting ahead of myself. The really notable fact was that somehow September arrived. We slogged through dust and heat and desertlands it seemed like forever, then it was September. The heat of the days was not as searing, and the nights became downright cold. We were in the Oregon Country, right enough, and we were making fourteen, fifteen, and sometimes even sixteen miles a day. Yet the trek never ended. The euphoria of winning the Snake contest wore off as our prize salmon disappeared into our stomachs. Oregon City itself seemed more like a dream than ever. It was a dream too far off—especially with winter cold closing in before we'd even gotten through the mild Indian summer of remembered New England autumns. The fact of the matter was, it wasn't even officially autumn yet, by the reckoning of a proper calendar.

Early one morning, I got to thinking about what date it truly was.

"Amelia?" I was finishing my dressing behind the wagon while she was considering two pairs of stockings in her hands.

"Do you think I should wear the summer stockings today, Phoebe? Or break in the winter ones?"

"Better save your woollies. It's not *that* cold yet." I began lacing my boots. "I mean, it's only September, I think. . . . You wouldn't happen to have any idea what part of September, would you?"

"Dates haven't crossed my mind since the Fourth of July, Phoebe. Not that I could ever forget *that* date." Amelia sighed and began pulling the summer stockings over her toes. "I suppose Miss Prendergast would know. She is the keeper of the books, the guardian of civilization—"

But I was already sprinting across the circle of wagons. How could I have forgotten that Miss Prendergast had also been keeping a calendar?

She was shaving Mr. Judd. He was perfectly capable of shaving himself long since, but as he appeared to be enjoying the attentions immensely, I didn't feel it was my place to comment upon that fact.

"Morning, Miss Prendergast, Mr. Judd."

Miss Prendergast turned from her labor of love inside the wagon and smiled. "Phoebe? You've been ignoring us of late."

"Not intentionally, ma'am. It just seems to be one thing after another, is all. Keeping Timothy from killing himself, for example."

"I thought dear Mr. Hawkins had the little ones under his wing."

"Well, he does, mostly, but Mr. Hawkins doesn't seem to care much for water. And there's been an awful amount of falls lately. Maybe it's the noise that hurts his head. I've watched him grab at his ears and run off each and every time we've gotten close to a waterfall."

"The poor man. I wonder if there's any cure at all for him. I've searched through all my herbals and even my *Indian Physician,* but alas, in vain." Miss Prendergast expertly caught the groove in Mr. Judd's chin with his razor, then sat back to admire her efforts as she wiped the blade clean of suds. She held up his little mirror. "Do you think the mustache could use the tiniest trim, Mr. Judd?"

"I kind of like it wild, Alice dear. I always used to think it gave me some protection from the hot fires I worked with. If I could smell whiskers burning, I knew I was too close. Not that I've been smithing for some time . . ." An expression of loss for his work crossed his face. "But if it would please you—"

"No, no, it shall remain as you prefer." She laid down her barbering tools and suddenly seemed to recall my presence. "May I help you with something, Phoebe? Or was this just a social visit?"

"Actually, Miss Prendergast, I was wondering if you could tell me the date. I've been a little concerned about how we're making time. And then again . . ." I wasn't going to say it, I really wasn't. Even bestowing a birthday kiss and hug as she always did, Mama might consider it an act of unwarranted pride. But it just slipped out. ". . . And then again, September just happens to be my birth month—"

Miss Prendergast dexterously slipped out from the whitetop. "How wonderful! We'll have something to celebrate!"

"Well, I can't say as how it's ever been really celebrated, and I certainly wasn't expecting anything. Still, it might be nice to know on the day—"

"Nonsense. Each and every one of us deserves to be remembered on our special day. And you particularly, Phoebe, for you've brightened the way for all of us." She walked over to her own wagon and shoved aside the faded cloth drooping from the rim of her whitetop. Then she paused to inspect a series of marks that had been etched upon the bent iron. "Now, what day of September, specifically?"

I stretched my neck to inspect Miss Prendergast's calendar system. It was neat and precise, like everything else she did. Weeks of seven days were divided into months, and each month marked, all the way back to Independence, Missouri. "Golly, but you've been busy!"

"So have we all, Phoebe. My busyness just matched my particular mind. I guess you could say this calendar is my own kind of elk skin. Yours did turn out beautifully . . . so soft and supple. I've been meaning to express my admiration. I believe it will be a much better remembrance of the trip than my poor efforts."

Not wanting Miss Prendergast to feel any worse for not having her very own elk skin, I blurted out the date. "September fifteenth. My birthday."

"Yes, of course." Miss Prendergast adjusted her spectacles and considered. "Why, there are but three days, Phoebe. Today is the twelfth!"

"Thank you, ma'am. I appreciate it."

I went off to help ready the oxen and consider. Only three days. I would be officially thirteen in three days. Practically grown up. Would I feel different?

Would my life change? I studied the Snake River, winding away from us to the north at Farewell Bend, the smaller Burnt River, which we would begin following west instead, and the Blue Mountains, hovering like a misty dream just beyond. In three days we'd be in those mountains; the first proper mountains of the entire trip that we couldn't easily avoid, the way South Pass had saved us from the Rockies.

For starters, my birthday looked to be a difficult traveling day. Difficult like my birth day, but different.

"Do watch how you swing that yoke, Phoebe. You nearly hit my head with it! Where is your mind?"

"Sorry, Amelia. I was busy cogitating on other things."

SEVEN

The Blue Mountains kept rising before us, growing larger and more impressive, until we were among them. We'd forgotten about high grades, and the tedious winching necessary to ease wagons down steep inclines. Our screaming muscles quickly reminded us. But we were all tougher now than earlier in the trip, thank heavens.

All except for Mabel Hatch. She must have been farther along in her pregnancy than even Happy Hawkins had estimated, for the woman could no longer pull and heave with us. It was almost too much for Mrs. Hatch to walk her oxen, straining as the baby was against her calico dress.

I was convinced it was going to be a good, healthy baby, even with Mabel so down at the mouth. It was being fed on lots of fresh air and O'Malley cow milk, wasn't it? The larger Mabel grew, the more fascinating the entire baby business became, at least to me. Maybe that had something to do with my own birthday coming on. Margaret said I was being silly.

"You'd think it was the next wonder of the world, the way you've been fussing over Mabel Hatch lately, Phoebe. Giving her an extra hand and all, even with all those other widows buzzing around her like bees at the hive."

I shrugged. "I've only been working up my nerve to ask if I could touch the baby, is all."

"What's to touch? It's got to be born first, hasn't it?"

"But does it move? Can she feel it?"

"Saints above! Of course she can feel it! Haven't you seen how she lurches every so often? That's the wee one giving her a proper kick, it is. It'll be a boy."

"How do you know?"

"Because boys are always anxious to get out and start in taking over the world. Girls can sense what's coming and are willing to wait."

Boy or no, I still longed for a touch. But Mabel Hatch wasn't truly the touching type. I consulted with Happy Hawkins. She slapped her ample thighs and laughed.

"Lordy, but you could have felt my stomach all you wanted in the old days, Phoebe. Five sons and a daughter I birthed joyfully. And each and every one of them a kicker." Then she shook her gray head and made sure Mabel was safely out of earshot. "You'll be touching the real thing sooner rather than later, I'm afeared. Let's hope she makes it to the Whitman Mission, at the least."

"But that's just to the other side of the Blue Mountains! The baby will come that soon?"

"With the Lord's help, it will then—and not by the great Columbia River. That river will be trial enough. As if we women haven't been tested already as bad as Job himself." Happy cast a glance at her poor husband hunched by a nearby campfire and shook her head. "Tested enough to deserve Willamette Valley's free land right this minute!"

"Will the Whitmans be able to aid Mrs. Hatch with the birthing?"

"They say Marcus Whitman is a doctor, and his wife Narcissa helps. Missionaries and healers both. They ought to be set up for any eventuality. They been out this way for ten years now, after all."

"I know. *We* heard about them clear back East— mainly on account of the Missionary Board regularly collecting funds at church to help them save the heathens."

Happy set off after her husband. "Don't play with that fire, Theodore! You'll hurt yourself!" She hauled him from the flames with practiced ease. "We'll see about the Whitmans by and by, Phoebe. First we've got to finish crossing these Blue Mountains!"

←—《 》—→

I didn't feel particularly different on the morning of my birthday. Maybe a little tired from all the winching the day before. There'd been one especially bad slope that had almost lost us Mama's cherrywood dresser. After lugging it around forever in the wagon, with Papa alternately talking to or cussing at it, that would have been a pity. I'd even begun to believe the thing was alive, the same as Papa.

He'd been in the way of cussing at it again this morning as we worked down a much easier hill.

"Blast!"

"What is it, Papa?"

"That confounded middle drawer of the top half, is what it is."

I groaned to myself. Papa's horizons had not been expanding with the scenery.

"It's the same confounded drawer that always swings out directly at my head. I swear, it's got it all planned out. A complete strategy!"

I hung on to Buck as he slid down the last ten feet of the slope. "Nonsense, Papa," I puffed, righting myself on the welcome flat stretch. "I wedged it shut myself this morning. *Tight* shut."

"It's a conspiracy! And my entire family is in on it, too!"

I glanced back at Mama on her wagon seat for a reaction. She was so used to this particular conversation that her head never even rose from the open Bible clasped tightly on her lap.

"Your grandmother Wintle never did want me to marry your mother," Papa ranted on. "She willed this monstrosity to us on purpose. I've been hearing that woman chuckling from the grave for months now—"

"That's just the wagon's natural traveling sounds, Papa."

"Get back. *Back!* Away from me, cursed fiend!"

Papa pounded at the drawer while I shook my head at my sister from across the oxen. Amelia merely shrugged. "The trip's become too long, Phoebe."

"I know."

When we stopped for the nooning in a sweet little valley filled with green grass, I'd about had enough of Papa's foul humor. Soon I'd be pulling at my ears the same as poor Mr. Hawkins. I set the oxen free to the grass and turned back to where Mama was trying her best to calm Papa.

"I'm just going to take the rifle up the next mountain a ways, Mama. Maybe find Mr. Harley's rabbit at long last. I need a little distance."

Mama pulled at her apron and made an ill-disguised face at the flimsy wall of our whitetop. "I can't say that I blame you, Phoebe. In fact, I'd like nothing better than to join you—"

"Don't you *dare* trot off on me, wife! Not until you've tended to the new bruises inflicted by your carnivorous keepsake!"

"Being *beaten* and being *eaten* are two separate things, Henry."

Papa ignored the distinction and drifted off into swear words again, and Mama sighed. I left Amelia taking her turn at fixing the meal to scamper off for an hour of blessed freedom.

Blissfully I headed up a slope into a thicket of trees. Peace at last. Just me and the rifle and the sound of birds and ground squirrels scurrying for early autumn feasts. And there were feasts to be had.

I soon realized I should have brought a pail instead of the rifle. Fat chokeberries and salmonberries were decorating shrubbery at every hand. I shoved a few of the tangy delicacies into my mouth as I considered. Return for a bucket or no? Puckering up on the not-quite-ripe berries, I heard other sounds through the trees ahead of me. Human sounds. Had we crossed paths with more Indians? Had the Mills Party bogged down ahead of us? We hadn't seen hide nor hair of them for ages, it seemed like.

Pushing very tentatively through the brush, I came upon a sight that set me to grinning. It wasn't either Indians or the Mills Party. Mr. Hawkins and the youngest O'Malleys had gone off foraging in advance of me. There, in a tiny open meadow, they were all giggling and stuffing themselves on berries as they worked down a row of wild bushes.

Mary Rose was singsonging a little ditty in between bites:

> *Berries red, have no dread,*
> *Berries white, poisonous sight.*
> *Leaves three, quickly flee.*

Mr. Hawkins, crouched low like the children, was humming tunelessly along with her. I stopped to check where my hands lay among the vines and creepers about me, just in case there might be some poison ivy about. There wasn't. I raised my head again and my lips were parted to greet them all when I noticed something else. My jaws clamped shut fast as I stiffened.

Working up the far end of the row, stuffing itself just as greedily, was a plump bear cub. A cute little thing it was, all fur and fat and shiny wet nose. Still and all, it was a *bear*. It was a *real* bear, not something I'd been making up in my hunting fantasies.

And in a moment, in only a moment, Timothy and the cub would be nose-to-nose.

It happened.

Both young cubs were slightly taken aback. The bear plunked down on its rump to one side, Timothy to the other. Timothy's curiosity got the better of him first. He raised a hand toward the cub. The cub raised a paw. Fingers and claws met. . . .

Maureen and Mary Rose O'Malley finally looked up. They shrieked. Behind them, Mr. Hawkins's face registered the situation with confusion. It was more than he could deal with.

I finally forced some words out of my throat. "Mary Rose. Maureen?" I spoke as calmly as I could, even though my heart had already slid clear down to my stomach. "Hush up and run away from there, before—" My eyes slid off the children as I heard the noise coming from behind the cub. Felt it, was more like it. I swear, the earth beneath my feet was shaking. Then came the other sound—the sound I had been dreading.

The growl of outrage.

Mr. Hawkins, the children, even the cub were frozen. My eyes moved up, and up, and up. Emerging from the forest to tower over all of them was another bear. A full-grown mama bear. A grizzly. She had to be. I'd never dreamed of any-thing so big, so *vast* . . . so *dangerous.*

No one budged, so I had to. I broke into the clearing, rifle before me. Was it loaded? Was it cocked? I couldn't remember.

"Timothy. Move. *Now.* Into the woods behind me. Maureen and Mary Rose. For the love of God, *move!*"

They came to life in slow motion. So did the mama grizzly. But for each five of their steps, she only needed one. Out of the corner of my eye I saw Mr. Hawkins standing to one side, still unable to function.

"Mr. Hawkins! *Please* move. I've got a gun. I'll protect the children. No! Don't go closer! Move away from her cub. She only wants her cub safe—"

But Mr. Hawkins was picking up a rock. *Don't throw that rock, Mr. Hawkins,* I pleaded silently. *Please, Lord, don't let him throw that rock!* The children were safely behind me, mama bear had reached her cub—

Mr. Hawkins threw the rock.

The giant grizzly had been stooped over her cub, sniffing for damage and grunting endear-ments. Now she brushed off the missile, rocked back on her hind legs, and rose once more. My, but she was glorious in her just fury! Eight full feet she must have stretched. Her huge golden-brown paws with their curved claws extended beyond; her open jaws flashed teeth long and sharp enough to behead anything in her way. And all that deadly magnificence was poised between Mr. Hawkins and *me*. *Me*. The fact hit home with sudden clarity.

"Why *me*? I'm just the peacemaker here, Mama Bear. There's no way I'd want to harm your baby. I *like* babies. . . ." Why was I talking out loud to that beast? But I kept on babbling as she focused her attention exclusively on myself. Maybe it was the gun. Could she know what a gun was?

"Don't pay any mind to this rifle. None at all. Why, until just a short time ago I couldn't have hit a barn broadside. And certainly not something that moved. I'm *positive* I couldn't hurt something that moves." I started backing away, rifle clutched in one arm too limp to even consider shooting. "Nice Mama Bear. Down, girl. . . ."

I backed until I could back no more. I'd backed right through the clearing and up against a tree trunk. And Mama Bear was lumbering closer and closer, dwarfing me. Only a few more steps and she'd have me surrounded by those great, outstretched arms. She'd have me caught in the embrace of those hairy paws and glinting claws.

This was not my idea of hunting.

I raised the rifle barrel again. I *had* loaded the gun. I must have.

A blur of motion diverted me from the gun.

"Mr. Hawkins! No!"

Mr. Hawkins was running in toward the bear's side, totally unarmed. Mama Bear stopped only long enough to swat him out of the way, as if she were ridding herself of a pesky fly.

Mr. Hawkins fell with a thud.

The sound of his head hitting hard rock was the last thing I heard before I aimed the rifle dead center on the bear and pulled the trigger.

The blast must have deafened me. And blinded me, too. I couldn't hear, couldn't see, and couldn't breathe. I was suffocating under a heavy, sticky blanket of fur. . . . Fur? I tried to feel with my fingers, but they were immovably pinned. So were my legs.

There could be only one explanation. My rifle *had* been loaded, and Mama Bear had expired upon me in all her towering majesty and weight. She was getting her final revenge.

Inconsequentially, I remembered the date. September fifteenth. My birthday. Mama had kissed and hugged me when I'd rolled out of my blankets this morning. After that my birthday had been promptly forgotten in the heaving of oxen and the skreaking of wagons as we all strained over the next piece of the Blue Mountains.

Thirteen. I had attained my thirteenth year. I moaned with sudden pity for myself, only to gag on a mouthful of fur. Miss Simpson would have to oversee my burial right here in the middle of the Blue Mountains. I hoped they would sink me deep enough so the wild creatures wouldn't be digging me up again. I hoped they'd all sing a pretty hymn, too. Not "Rock of Ages," either. I didn't think I could stand "Rock of Ages" after singing it at those buffalo massacre burials. . . . Mama would surely erect some kind of a marker, wouldn't she? At least a little wooden cross. And Amelia, my lovely big sister Amelia. If Miss Simpson would let the wagons lay over, Amelia would probably compose a verse or two for me. Surely she'd make that effort.

After all that, what then? Would my soul be stuck here in the Blue Mountains forever? The way Yellow Feather's first sister's soul seemed to be marooned atop Scotts Bluff? Would I be howling like the wolves every time a living human crossed my path? For eternity?

I snuffled to myself. I'd never see Oregon proper. Even worse, the world would never know what they'd lost in Phoebe Brown.

Thirteen. It was too young to die. I blubbered into the fur and blacked out.

"Phoebe . . . Phoebe! . . . Oh, wake up, dear sister!"

Voices were calling from a very great distance. I listened to them, smiling in my head, not quite willing to leave the place of infinite quiet and peace that I seemed to have stumbled upon.

"Phoebe! . . . It's Mama, Phoebe. . . . I didn't bring you into this world thirteen years ago to lose you in the wilderness to a bear! . . . Phoebe, darling, come back!"

One eye creaked open. It was like at the beginning of the world, when God said, "Let there be light." There *was* light. "Mama?"

Mama's dark hair was askew and there were tears streaming down her face. "Phoebe! My little girl! Are you truly alive? Can you move?"

Must've been a few muscles working, at least, because I stretched a finger to reach for my mother's damp face, then my own. "I think so, Mama. Just . . . a little groggy . . . Are the children saved? Is Mr. Hawkins all right?"

Mr. Hawkins quite unexpectedly loomed into my view and answered for himself. "I'm right as rain. It's you needs tending, young miss."

I guess I *was* in a state, because I never questioned the fact that it was *Mr. Hawkins* saying those things. But I did notice that for the first time in nearly half a year, a man took over. Strong arms lifted me and tenderly bore me down the mountain slope to the valley. I was laid on a bed of blankets by a fire and Happy Hawkins gave me a good going over. It must have been hard for her to concentrate. There were tears in her own eyes the whole time as she glanced between me and her husband.

"Heaven knows how you did it, Phoebe Brown. Praise the Lord! You've restored my Theodore to me! Just as good as new he and his head are. I find one bone broken in this body, it's me that'll carry you on my back—clear to Oregon City!"

But even Happy Hawkins's enthusiastic ministrations could find no broken bones, only numbness. I tried to raise my head. It hurt. Still, I was able to take in the entire train poised breathless above my resting place. There were the twins, wide-eyed, and Margaret O'Malley, so pale that her freckles had nearly disappeared from her cheeks. Between them, Miss Prendergast was dabbing tears from her spectacles.

"Happy birthday, Phoebe dear," she whispered.

Well, I guess it was a happy birthday, after all. I was still alive, wasn't I? There couldn't be any greater present than that.

I closed my eyes and drifted back into sleep.

EIGHT

"*A*re your jaws too sore, Phoebe, or can you handle this bear liver? Mama fried it in *real butter* from the O'Malleys' cow!"

"I guess I could give it a try, Amelia." It was my turn to be propped against a wagon wheel, recuperating.

"Drink some milk, Phoebe!" Timothy O'Malley thrust a cup at me. Only a little spilled.

"I've pegged out the bear skin for you, Phoebe. Mama helped. To give you a start on the tanning when you're feeling better."

This heroine business had its merits. I wondered how long it could last. "Why, thank you, Amelia. Did you save the head, too? I hope you saved the head. It was powerful."

"I did. But my, such teeth! And did you see the size of those paws, Phoebe? And the claws!" Amelia's eyes burned with the thrill of it all.

"In passing, Amelia. In passing." It was easy enough for my sister to build a romantic view of the whole affair. She hadn't been at the trouble end of those paws and claws. I shifted my body very tentatively. It still felt like one of Mama's prize jellied aspics, even after I'd slept all night and half of this day, as well. "Miss Simpson wasn't too angry with me, Mama?"

"She took her share of the bear meat like everyone else. She even laid over a whole day for you, Phoebe. That's saying a lot."

"Not to mention that this valley has the best grass we've seen in months." Amelia brought me back to reality as only a sister could. "The animals are in heaven."

I turned to my father, sprawled against the far wheel. "How was the bear steak, Papa?"

"A mite tough, but acceptable, daughter."

I sighed. "What will become of that poor little orphaned grizzly cub?"

I had the time to work through my rescue as I sat on the wagon seat next to Mama for the next few days as the oxen heaved first up, then down the remaining mountains. I was allover bruised even worse than that time Happy Hawkins had accidentally stomped on me back in Pawnee country—and too weak in the knees yet to do any steady walking. It was truly amazing how much an eight-hundred-pound bear could crush out of a body.

I still wasn't sure why I was considered the heroine of the adventure. It was the little O'Malleys who'd really done the rescuing. Once I'd chased them from danger they'd gone barreling down the mountain screaming bloody murder. By the time the entire camp of women had run back up the mountain, wielding guns and knives, Mr. Hawkins was just rising from where the bear had flung him. He was dripping blood from an impressive set of claw marks on one side of his face, and rubbing at the back of his skull.

Miraculously, he was also perfectly sane and clearheaded. He could remember nothing of the months since the buffalo massacre, but was able to recount the entire bear episode as if he'd been standing back and watching the whole thing. What he mostly kept saying, though, was, "Never saw nothing like the way that Phoebe girl stood up to that bear." It was getting embarrassing. Almost. What had he expected me to do? Swoon away like Sarah Kennan in the old days? I had done that, of course, but not when it mattered. Not when it was just Mama Grizzly and me, nose-to-nose.

Once it had been verified that the monumental grizzly was, indeed, dead, and that I was underneath her, the obstacle had been removed.

"Well, I guess I got my bear, whether I truly

wanted her or not. And here I am," I muttered aloud.

"What's that, Phoebe?"

"Nothing much, Mama. I suppose I'm just happy to be all in one piece. Why, in a few days, when my bruises stop looking putrid, it'll be as if it never happened. Not that I'll ever wish for bears again. Should have stuck to rabbit hunting from the start, like Mr. Harley recommended. Nice, safe little jackrabbits."

Mama shuddered. "I'll fear that bear till my dying day. I haven't even worked out yet how I'm going to live with that grizzly skin of yours. When a mother sees her child in such danger . . . I would have murdered that creature with my bare hands, Phoebe, if you hadn't already done the deed."

"I think I understand a little more about that now, Mama. Mama Grizzly felt that way too."

But my own mother had no fellow feelings to spare for the dead beast. She was suddenly half rising from the wagon seat. "Look, Phoebe! We've come to the end of the Blue Mountains at last!"

I looked. Our wagon hovered on a final bluff of the dry, treeless side of the range. Spread below us were miles of flatlands, clear into the horizon. Somehow the Petticoat Party had made it to the final leg of the journey.

When we pulled into the Whitman Mission, we were in finer fettle than we'd been in months. Miss Simpson herself had called it a *catalyst,* that bear incident. She explained in her best schoolteacher style. It meant one event causing other events to just start happening.

Since my bear had clonked Mr. Hawkins, restoring him to his right mind, our other male invalids had perked up remarkably. Papa and Mr. Judd were clamoring to be let out of their wagons to test their legs. Mr. O'Malley had actually pulled his own self onto solid ground that very morning, if not for long. I'd been well enough by then to stumble over to the O'Malleys' when I heard the entire family screeching at him. Those O'Malleys did tend to live at the top of their lungs.

"Merciful heavens! Back into your bed, Gerald!"

"Da! Da! You'll wreck yourself!"

"It's nothing of the sort I'll be doing!" Mr. O'Malley was in his long red underwear—pink since his bath in the therapeutic springs—clutching on to the rear of the wagon for dear life. Tufts of carroty curls screwed out from his head in every direction. He puffed and huffed, more crimson-faced than usual. "I've just got to find my land legs again, is all."

"When we get to the mission, husband, we'll have you properly examined. You, and the others, too. Dr. Whitman will be the judge!"

Mr. O'Malley was packed back into the wagon, fighting every inch of the way.

We were expecting maybe a full-blown city, with a proper hospital and everything, after all those free-will missionary donations to the Whitmans. What we found was a handful of modest, low adobe buildings without a stockade or any other protection from the Cayuse Indians the Whitmans had come to minister.

Papa peeked out the window he'd carved in our whitetop a day or two back when he was feeling particularly feisty. I watched him take in the flat land between a few bald, parched hills. Together we studied a brown garden surrounded by dry grasses. Next, the flowing, unmown grass that led to a narrow river with a pent-up pond next to a small mill. There were ducks swimming in the pond.

"Graft!" Papa exclaimed. "All those pennies we contributed must be feathering the Mission Board's pockets!"

"Nonsense, Henry," Mama replied. She'd slipped alongside and had been examining the spread next to us. "It appears to be a lovely job done with what's available. The Whitmans are merely the first missionaries in the Oregon Country. What about financing our missions to the poor starving Chinese? Or all those naked Hawaiian Islanders needing to be clothed? What about—"

Luckily this discussion was terminated by the arrival of the Whitmans themselves—and what appeared to be the entire population of their establishment, Indians and children included. They all seemed genuinely delighted to greet us.

"Welcome to Waiilatpu!" That was Dr. Whitman. He was tall, with a strong, hooked nose presiding over a full mustache and carefully trimmed chin beard. He wasn't any stranger to hard labor, either. Shirtsleeves rolled above bronzed, hardened arms gave proof of that.

"We thank the Lord you have arrived before the snows." Mrs. Whitman was an attractive woman in her late thirties. Her light brown hair was parted in the center and twisted back from her face. She was smiling at us, but her eyes were sad. Miss Prendergast told me that Mrs. Whitman had been the very first white woman to cross the plains, a full ten years ago. Maybe that had done something to her. Maybe our own crossing had changed the way we women looked, too.

"But where are your men?" Mrs. Whitman's question brought me back to the present. "Unless . . . the Mills Party that came this way but a week past talked of an extraordinary train of women—"

Miss Simpson surged forward and held out her firm, sun-browned hand. "I'm Emily Simpson, and this is my group—"

"The Petticoat Party?" asked Mrs. Whitman. The smile reached her eyes this time. "Why, then, you are doubly welcome. We have been praying for your safe arrival these past days! You must come and dine with us this evening, Miss Simpson. We would know of your every travail, and how you overcame."

"Just leave your wagons in a line where they are, Miss Simpson," added Dr. Whitman. "You've nothing to fear from our good Cayuse here."

"Thank you, Doctor, but if you would be so kind . . ." As she was our leader, Miss Simpson got to do the dining, but she also had to do the begging. "We are not solely without male accompaniment. In fact, our last three invalids are awaiting your attentions in their wagons, if we might ask your services—"

My, but she'd done that politely. Not our usual brash Miss Simpson at all. Were the beginnings of civilization affecting her?

"Dear lady, it would be my pleasure to tend to your men, to be of some real help. I cannot conceive how it happens, but my Indians are hard to cure. They die from ailments which are mere childhood diseases to us—measles or the mumps." Dr. Whitman rubbed an arm over his forehead. "And then they would rather take their ills to a witch doctor."

"Have you conferred with these witch doctors? Some native methods are strangely effective."

I could tell our leader was working up a scientific interest in this new subject. *She* would've bearded a wild witch doctor any day of the week.

"In what language, Miss Simpson? They'll not learn English, and I'll not learn their tongue until accommodation is made. And few of the Cayuse wish to accommodate."

Miss Simpson was startled. "Does that not make preaching the Word difficult, Dr. Whitman?"

"Near impossible, my dear lady, near impossible. But we have the emigrants like you to tend now, coming more each year—" He stopped. "Enough. Let me see to your patients while the light is yet strong."

I'd been standing quietly in the background, listening to all this. I turned to my sister. "Ten years, Amelia. I could've learned Sioux, or even Snake, in a couple of months. What kind of accommodation is that?"

"Hush, Phoebe. We don't want to insult the Whitmans. But it is curious."

There were lots of curious things about that mission. For one thing, there were only about a dozen converted Cayuse. It seemed like a mighty small congregation for ten years' labor in the fields of the Lord.

I was downright grateful I didn't feel the Calling, like Mrs. Whitman had. It must be awful being stuck out here forever in this dry place—so close, yet so far from the promised greenery of the Willamette Valley ahead. Also, over the months I'd learned to like Indians just fine, and admire them and their way of doing things, too. If they figured their Great Spirit was good enough for them, why force them into other ways and names for God?

Aside from the Indian business, the local children were a little peculiar, too. Maybe it was because of how strict they were being raised. That was easy to tell on account of how they held back from us—shy, yes, but mostly stiff and a little scared. Some belonged to parents that ran an outlying mission, but a bunch of them were part of the Sager family.

Those Sagers didn't talk much, but they did say enough to let on they were orphaned on the trail two years back. Their father and mother had died hardly a month apart—one of camp fever, the other from childbirthing. Those seven Sagers, baby and all, had somehow made it over the Blue Mountains, and the Whitmans had adopted them. One of the Sager girls allowed as how that had come to pass because Dr. and Mrs. Whitman's own little daughter, Alice, had just died of drowning, right there in that innocent-looking mill pond. The one with all the ducks in it. No wonder Mrs. Whitman had that sad look.

After I dug as much out of the Sagers as they were willing to share, I headed back to the wagons, thinking maybe there were worse things that could have happened to our party. I was also itching to hear Dr. Whitman's diagnosis of Papa's state of fitness. I'd been delighted when Mr. Hawkins had been so surprisingly restored to health. But then, Mr. Hawkins had always been Happy's lookout, and never much of a trouble to the rest of the train, before or after the buffalo massacre. Mr. Judd was another quiet man who kept his own counsel. Papa and Mr. O'Malley were different kettles of fish entirely.

We girls had gotten somewhat accustomed to running things on our own. It was long months since the O'Malleys or Amelia and I had acted on any of the advice flowing freely from the invalids sheltered within our two family whitetops.

There was Miss Simpson to consider, too. She'd done a fair job of pulling us all together since the buffalo massacre, and of keeping us that way. Papa's first act upon his recovery would likely be a mutiny attempt against her. It wasn't in his nature to be ruled by a woman. That was another good reason to keep him in the wagon till the end of the line.

It wasn't what I feared might happen if Papa won. More like what might happen if he didn't.

Blind to all but these considerations, I barged directly into Margaret outside the O'Malley wagon.

"Sorry, Margaret—"

"Shhh, Phoebe. I'm trying to hear what Dr. Whitman is saying to Da!"

"Oh. Is he still here? And what happened with Mr. Judd?"

"It's the wagon for him till Oregon City." Margaret put a finger to her lips and we both listened.

"That must have been quite a buffalo you came up against, Mr. O'Malley. Quite a herd. You must be thanking God every day for your deliverance, and the care of your women. Your wound was akin to open surgery." There was a pause. Dr. Whitman was probably prodding the wound in question. "Need I add that it's a rare man that survives open surgery in a hospital, no less in the dust of the Oregon Trail?"

"Ouch. Watch those fingers, Doctor, if you please. It's the saints themselves preserved me. The saints and my old woman dousing me wound with hard whiskey thrice the day. And never a drop crossed my parched lips, more's the pity!"

Margaret grinned at that, but Dr. Whitman seemed less amused. "A novel therapy. I'd take note if the demon rum were not forbidden to me and mine."

"That'd be a true hardship, Doctor . . . ouch!"

Dr. Whitman began edging from the wagon. "It's healing, but I'd not strain the wound, Mr. O'Malley. Oregon City will be soon enough to exert yourself. And from there I'd recommend you work at half strength for another month."

This was not what Mr. O'Malley wished to hear. His thanks did not follow the doctor's exit. Mrs. O'Malley fulsomely made up for the deficit, however.

Margaret jabbed me, her relief evident.

"So that's what became of your share of Captain Kennan's jugs!"

"Sure enough." Margaret grinned. "And my ma

bought more at Laramie and Fort Bridger. It's been the very devil keeping those lips of Da's parched, though!"

I shook my head and followed Dr. Whitman to our own wagon. The prognosis there was better for Papa, but worse for my comfort of mind. In a surprisingly short time the doctor was giving Mama instructions.

"He may begin taking the air daily, Mrs. Brown. Probably only during stops for another week. Your husband will need to strengthen his leg muscles and relearn how to walk. I'll have someone send over a pair of crutches for his support—"

"Damned if I'll hobble around like a cripple!" Papa yelled from the wagon.

I watched Dr. Whitman's face turn severe. "Your legs will be damned without, Mr. Brown. Put too much weight on those fractures until your muscles have strengthened and you'll find yourself a cripple for life!"

My father shut up. Maybe I needn't worry about planning a Papa strategy after all. That threat of being crippled for life should be enough to keep him off Miss Simpson's back for another few weeks. Just long enough to see us safely to Oregon City.

NINE

*M*iss Simpson gathered our party together after she returned from her supper with the Whitmans that evening.

"Ladies—" she began, then noticed Mr. Hawkins. "*Friends.* I know we'd planned to lay over for a day here at the mission, but in my talk with the Whitmans I learned somewhat of the rigors still before us."

"What more can still face us, Emily?" Miss Prendergast seemed worried behind her spectacles.

"You've got a guidebook too, Alice. You know about the mountains and the river."

"It sure would be easier if we could just boat down that Columbia," Happy Hawkins ventured.

"Easier, true. Our animals are nearly exhausted. One option the Whitmans mentioned was to stop and build boats at Fort Walla Walla, and send our animals overland by Indian guides. However—" Miss Simpson stopped at the sudden buzz around her, waiting for it to settle. "However. We have neither the strength nor the knowledge to be boat building."

The buzz rose again.

"Ladies, please. We must accept our limitations and live with them."

"That wasn't what you said back on the plains after the buffalo massacre!"

"No. It certainly was not!"

"Mrs. Davis. Mrs. Kincaid. I'll be the first to admit we've overcome much and grown much since that lamentable occasion. I'll also be the first to admit that being forced to think like a man does not give us the physical strength of one. The building of boats is out of the question. Neither have we the money to be buying boats from the fort."

"Tell us what that leaves us, Miss Simpson. Please."

It was Mabel Hatch, arms folded over her pregnant stomach. The baby appeared about ready to pop out any second, but hadn't chosen to ease things by doing so at the mission.

"Unfortunately, Mrs. Hatch, that means we must walk the final distance along the Columbia as far as the Dalles. From that point, the Whitmans inform me, the trail becomes too treacherous through the Cascade Mountains. We must detour along the newly constructed Barlow Road. A toll road."

Her last words caused more stricken looks. Money was scarce as hen's teeth in the party.

Everyone was trying to save some for the arriving.

"Moreover," Miss Simpson continued, "the snows will begin in the next few weeks. We cannot afford to be caught in the mountains when that happens. It might be disastrous."

Snow. I gulped. Here I'd just been worrying over dealing with Papa, forgetting about the snow. I glanced around. Even in the twilight, the mission fields seemed brittle with dryness and heat. That heat had come on strong again as soon as we'd left the Blue Mountains. It was hard to even picture snow. A few weeks? That estimation had to be ridiculous.

"Surely the Whitmans were exaggerating?" Mrs. Russell voiced my thoughts.

"It cannot be!" Tabitha Kennan looked to be working herself up again.

"Please." Miss Simpson interrupted the women. "Ten years the Whitmans have lived here. Their advice has to be accepted. We've no other sources. In view of that, we'd best be on our way at first light. It's three days to the Hudson's Bay Company's outpost at Walla Walla, and then we take on the cliffs of the Columbia."

Her duty completed, Miss Simpson strode off for her wagon. We girls dallied for a while, commiserating.

"Pooh!" exclaimed Hannah Kennan. "Those Sager boys, John and Frank? They were going to sneak out of school to show sister and me a real Cayuse village tomorrow."

"How'd you get the Sager boys to talk like that?" I asked. "They ignored me entirely. And their sisters seemed too scared to say much. It was harder than pumping from a dry well, getting anything out of them."

"They were under orders from their schoolmaster," Hannah explained. "He and the Whitmans don't want them getting too friendly with us wagon train people."

"They're afraid we might upset their Christian upbringing." Sarah tossed a golden plait and giggled. "Can you imagine? Hannah and I as moral distractions?"

Lizzie O'Malley made a face. "How old are those Sager boys? About fifteen and sixteen by the looks of them. Only too easily, Sarah. Only too easily."

"Well, la-de-da." It was Sarah's turn to make a face. "I'm going to get some beauty sleep regardless. Perhaps Miss Simpson will change her mind in the morning. Who ever heard of snow at the end of September? Are you coming, Hannah?"

Miss Simpson's mind remained unchanged. Shortly after daybreak our wagons were on the trail again. After three days of sweltering heat as fierce as any we had met going through desert and bad-lands, we arrived at Fort Walla Walla.

The fort was another stockaded outpost for fur trading, set on the very bank of the great Columbia River. It wasn't much of a sight. That was mainly because we arrived in the middle of a raging dust storm, and grit-filled winds hid most of the barren lands from our view.

"Amelia!" My sister was but a few yards to the other side of the oxen, but it was impossible yelling through the cloth wrapped around my nose and mouth. "Amelia!" The blast tore my words away. "We have to circle the wagons tighter! I said tighter . . . wagons *closer!* Could be some protection—"

Alas, there was little protection to be found for us. There was even less for the poor miserable oxen after Amelia and Mama and I finally managed— hunched over and half stumbling from the onslaught—to set them free. There was nothing but sand for their mouths, and they'd need to wait for the winds to die before they could even find the river's water.

I felt a little sorry for us, too. And I wasn't the only one. Amelia and Mama and I met up with the other women in the center of our makeshift barricade against the elements.

"Mercy!" Mrs. O'Malley unraveled her scarf to spit like a trooper. "If it isn't Injuns we're needing to blockade against, it's sand. And here we've come almost to the end of our journey. Sure and there can't be more than two hundred miles to travel, can there?"

Happy Hawkins finished the thought. "And our promised land turns to dust and grit before our eyes."

Mabel Hatch lurched and clutched at her stomach. "There is no hope for us! No hope for my poor, fatherless baby! All this way, and for what?"

"Dust!" Miss Simpson cleared her mouth of the word distastefully, then rushed to protect her face again. Her muffled words still came through. "No point in even considering supper, ladies. Who wants to eat a plateful of dust?"

After this pronouncement, she hauled off Happy and her husband. Together they fought the wind to visit Walla Walla for further advice. Papa didn't even consider taking his daily exercise on the despised crutches. He remained within his walls of canvas, not complaining, for once, about the now sheltering cherrywood dresser. As for Amelia and

Mama and me, we crawled under the meager sanctuary of the wagon and buried our heads in our blankets.

In the morning I emerged from under the wagon to shake dust from every crease of my clothing, to brush grit from every pore of my skin. I had to wash my eyes out three times before I could believe what I was seeing.

I had awakened to a new world. The wind had stilled. The sky was cloudless and clear. The barren sand took on a rosy hue as rays of the rising sun touched it. The Columbia River itself—almost frighteningly close to our camp of wagons—cut through this glowing desert with an incredible strength.

I'd seen great rivers before, but the Mississippi had been only sprawling and muddy. The Columbia was different. It was wide, and it was deep and it was blue. It was sheer, exhilarating power. It carved its way through the landscape, heeding nothing—it definitely knew where it was going.

I let out a whistle of admiration. That river was challenging me, sure as I was standing there; almost as if I were an equal. Suddenly I knew if I were ever to meet a young man as deep and strong as that river, a young man who'd challenge me as an equal, I'd be just as lost as Amelia. It was a novel thought for someone of my former convictions. It startled me more than the footsteps coming from behind.

"Phoebe?" Amelia had almost caught up with me. "Phoebe, you haven't forgotten it's your turn to cook breakfast, have you? And it will have to be a big one after going to sleep hungry last night in that dreadful . . . Oh." She stopped. "Oh! What I wouldn't give to ride down that. In a boat, a raft, a canoe. *Anything*."

That river was working its strange magic on both of us. "It would be something, wouldn't it."

"More than something. It would be *thrilling*."

The cliffs that erupted to either side of the Columbia seemed to snap into tighter focus.

"Did you see that, Amelia? The cliffs are daring us too. Saying we haven't the nerve. Can't do it their way."

Amelia studied those cliffs. "There were trees there once, Phoebe. Look at the stumps. Some even seem freshly cut. I'll bet the Mills Party chopped down the last of them for *their* boats. I think the cliffs are just angry. It's far harder to despoil the river."

Then she shook herself. "Listen to us, both acting as if the river and cliffs are alive—"

"They might be, Amelia." It was hard, but I tore my eyes from the sight, buried my inexplicable thoughts, and readied myself for breakfast duty.

The Mills Party *had* been the villains responsible for the demise of the last stand of trees by Fort Walla Walla. They'd chopped wood, constructed rafts, and floated down the Columbia all within a week, leaving but the day before our own arrival. Why I thought of them as villains was unclear. If we'd the manpower and had gotten to Walla Walla first, we'd have done the same. Maybe it had something to do with Amelia's still being upset about that young printer from their party.

With those insights the Columbia had left fresh within me, I took a chance and brought up the subject as we badgered the oxen up the first slope taking us to the cliff trail that followed the south side of the Columbia.

"You think you'll see him again in Oregon City, Amelia?"

"Who?"

"You know, that printer. Wade Jethro?"

"Jennings!"

"Pardon me." I'd known it was Jennings all along, but couldn't help testing her. He'd looked presentable enough to me that night back at Independence Rock, but nowhere near deep and strong enough for my requirements. Fortunately, I was in no hurry to meet those requirements. With Amelia getting on in age the way she was, though, her interest was beginning to make more sense. I paced through a few minutes of silence. "Think he'll really start up a newspaper?"

"*The Oregon Intelligencer.* He'd already worked out a name for it. . . . Oh, Phoebe, to be bringing the printed word to the wilderness—"

"Yes?"

Her ox stumbled and she waited for him to find his footing again. "—I just cannot conceive of anything as *romantic*!"

I had other thoughts about that, but forbore expressing them.

Amelia rambled on. "It will be a weekly at first, and Wade can support it by selling advertisements and doing small jobs of printing on the side—"

"Wade? Does that mean you've forgiven him?"

"I haven't seen him to forgive him, Phoebe. And I'm still not sure that I shall. . . . Perhaps our paths will never even cross. Ever again."

That last note was so despondent that I couldn't

help but try to cheer her. "How many people could live in Oregon City? I mean, even if it's called a *city*, it couldn't be much more than a village, could it? Only consider how everything else out here has been exaggerated."

We'd finally huffed to the top of the rocky cliff. We paused for a moment to gaze down into the mighty Columbia, so far below.

"The *wilderness* hasn't been exaggerated, Phoebe. Only the sorry efforts of man to overcome it."

The deep blue ribbon of river surged on. For once my sister was absolutely right.

TEN

$\mathcal{I}$t was a hundred and thirty miles as the crow flies from Fort Walla Walla to the Dalles. The Dalles was where we'd find our cutoff onto the Barlow Road that would take us around Mount Hood to Oregon City. We weren't crows, more's the pity. We weren't making any fifteen miles a day on the treacherous trail above the Columbia River, either. During the course of the next two weeks we were fortunate if we made eight or ten.

The weather got cooler and cooler, while gradually the land changed from desert to copses of trees, and finally into forest. It was real forest. It even had oaks like the ones back in Massachusetts, until the evergreens started taking over. Those evergreens were giants, dwarfing us and the wagons, too. Beneath their constant brooding presence it became impossible to remember the time back on the plains when we'd cried for the sight of trees.

And all this way the Columbia River rolled on to our right, breaking into falls and whirlpools that increased my admiration of its incredible strength, but made me almost glad we hadn't gotten boats after all. Some kinds of masculinity could be too powerful.

"How do you suppose the Mills Party got past all those rocks and raging waters in their rafts?" I asked Amelia one day.

"I guess they'd have to portage. They'd unload everything off the rafts, carry the supplies around the falls overland, then repack again for the next stretch of the river."

"They'd carry the rafts too?"

"Don't ask me, Phoebe. Ask Miss Prendergast. She seems to know about everything else."

That night after supper I did. Miss Prendergast was discussing Mount Hood with Mr. Judd while she waited outside his wagon window to retrieve his supper dishes.

"Only imagine, Mr. Judd. Mount Hood has a conelike shape because it's a dead volcano. And it's over eleven thousand feet high, according to the calculations of explorers in my books. Snow stays upon its peak the entire year!"

"Just so we don't encounter any of that snow around its base, Alice." He handed her his tin plate and I could see him pull at his quilt. "Feels like it's freezing already."

Miss Prendergast tightened the shawl around her shoulders. Involuntarily, I did the same with mine. It was getting colder. It wasn't my imagination. I glanced up at the night sky. The days were shorter now, too. Already the moon was up, with a kind of filmy halo of clouds forming around it.

"About portaging, Miss Prendergast?"

"Phoebe!" She started. "You're here?"

"Yes, ma'am. I am, indeed." I launched into my question.

"They hire the Indians, dear. Flatheads, I believe. For a few twists of tobacco they actually lower the rafts and boats over the falls. As I understand it, for a few more twists, they'll carry all the supplies on portage too."

"Oh. That sounds so simple. . . . But I don't think I've heard tell of these Flatheads yet. What exactly does the name signify?"

"Again, according to my books, exactly what it says. Their heads are flattened as infants. It's considered a form of beauty. Would you care for another cup of coffee, Mr. Judd? To warm you for the night?"

"Don't mind if I do, Alice. If it's not too much trouble—"

"No trouble at all, Mr. Judd."

I left Miss Prendergast to her ministrations and

wandered back to our own wagon. Papa was jumping around it in circles on his crutches. At least that's what it looked like. He was getting quite proficient in his labors, with no signs of crippling whatsoever. But he hadn't taken on Miss Simpson yet. Maybe he figured he had to be solidly on his own two feet before he did that. I surely would want to be.

"Coming along fine, Papa."

His face was beaded with sweat in the cold night air. "Thank you, daughter. Glad to see someone take notice of my efforts."

"Why, Henry, I complimented you not five minutes ago," Mama said.

"Five minutes of this torture requires more than one compliment, Ruth."

I caught Mama crack a small smile behind Papa's back. "I'll keep that in mind, Henry. It's a shame you didn't allow me to pack my sand clock for this journey. I could have timed the compliments for three minutes, like a perfectly done egg."

Papa growled and stumped around behind the wagon again. I threw a few logs on the fire and settled near its warmth with my blankets.

There was a fine layer of hoarfrost crusting everything in the morning. The blankets snapped and crinkled as I crawled out from them. I turned my face toward the sky, hunting for signs of the sun, and was rewarded with a fine haze of freezing mist. On closer examination I found the entire encampment fogged in.

"Son of a gun!" I got up and immediately bumped into Amelia.

"Watch where you're going, Phoebe!"

"Pardon me. It's not my fault some cloud fell on us during the night."

It truly had. It was impossible to see anything more than a few feet in any direction. "How are we going to walk along the trail in this? We'd walk right over the edge into the Columbia."

"We're not." Happy Hawkins's voice came through the fog. "Miss Simpson sent me around to give everyone notice. Take your time with breakfast, because we can't go anywhere right now."

Who needed breakfast? I crawled back into my blankets, frost and all.

That cloud cost us an entire day. The next one was cold and rainy and we moved, but by nightfall half the wagon train was coughing and snuffling. It was the worst for Mabel Hatch. Each time she coughed, she grabbed at her stomach, like it hurt. Would that baby never come? Maybe it was only waiting for better weather.

At least Mabel was traveling inside her wagon now, instead of out, for Mr. Hawkins had graciously taken over her team. He'd tried to give his wife a rest just after he'd gotten well again, but Happy told him she was too used to the work and anyhow there wasn't any point in coddling *her*. Happy was probably correct.

The weather finally cleared and warmed a little when we made the Dalles. You couldn't miss the Dalles. To the one side was a tiny Methodist mission of a few buildings, and to the other was a great chasm in the Columbia through which torrents poured quite ferociously over boulders. In between was a Flathead fishing village of rickety shacks. That's where I finally learned about head flattening.

We arrived late in the afternoon, having spent all of the previous day surviving a difficult crossing of the Deschutes River where it surged over the trail and into the Columbia. I was feeling a little peevish. The exertions were getting no easier as we closed in on our goal. Sandstorms, fog, and frigid rain; nasty, raging rivers. When would the elements let up on us? It was almost as bad as Mabel Hatch waiting for her baby. Would the end never come? Suddenly Timothy was tugging at me.

"Phoebe! Phoebe!"

I brushed him off. "Not now, Timothy. Go torture your sisters."

"They sent me after you! Come see!"

"What?"

He shoved a small freckled fist into his forehead and pantomimed a drooling baby. "Injuns, Phoebe. Funny ones!"

"Oh, all right." With little grace I followed him from the camp to the Flathead huts. There I found the O'Malley girls clustered to the rear of a shack, staring. And well they might.

"Goodness! What's she done to that baby!"

It was immediately evident what a Flathead was. A mother of the species squatted next to a fire, smoking fish. Her head was flattened back to a point, leaving her with a long, sloping forehead. And that forehead was allover tattooed with exotic designs. More frightening than her visage, though, was the infant lying on the ground next to her. I gulped. The little thing was tightly bound to a board, and there were two more boards fastened at a sharp angle over its head.

It was being flattened. *Squished*. Right before my eyes.

"Isn't that amazing, Phoebe?" Margaret breathed.

I backed away. "Don't anybody let Mabel Hatch come near this village. She'd get sick."

I felt sick myself and dashed toward the nearest cliff for some privacy. There was a chair-size boulder next to the edge and I sank upon it gratefully. I spent some moments contemplating the churning waters of the cataracts before me—tumbling seemingly hundreds of feet into the chasm below—while my mind churned just as fast.

How many different kinds of Indians had we met on this trip? There'd been the tame ones back in Independence, Missouri, to begin with. Then the Pawnee who'd fallen head over heels for the Kennan twins. The only other tribes had been my Sioux and the Snakes. The Cayuse didn't count, at least not the converted ones we'd seen. They were almost as pitiful as the tame ones back in Independence.

But all those wild kind of Indians had been, well, exhilarating. Every bit as exhilarating as the wildness of the land itself. The memory of the way they dressed and the sounds of their drums and their languages swept over me. There were still plenty on the train who considered them either heathens or animals, though. In my mind they could never be either.

My thoughts naturally turned to my little Sioux blood brother, Yellow Feather. Had he bagged any more elk? Had he grown? Had he steered clear of swimming in the Platte River? . . . And Red Fish of the Snakes. Maybe he'd trick some other emigrant party out of rifles and a horse. I kind of hoped he would.

My Indian friends had been bright-eyed and clever and vibrant with *life*. That was what was troubling me, without doubt. The Flathead mother's eyes had been vacant, almost dead. Her baby's, too. Had their brains been squeezed right out of existence by those wretched boards?

I reached up a finger to scratch at my neck just as Timothy wandered by.

"What's the matter, Phoebe? You scared of them Injuns? You're allover gray, same color as that rock you're on!"

I glanced down at the boulder. It was gray. More unusual, my rock was *moving*. So was my blue calico dress. Only it wasn't blue anymore. Curious. I shifted my skirt deliberately. The whole color scheme shifted with it. Then the bites began. Straight up my legs and arms to my neck.

"Yipes! I'm crawling! I'm allover crawling with fleas!"

Margaret dashed into view, thinking Timothy was going over the falls. "Saints preserve us! Shake 'em off, Phoebe!"

I shook, and Margaret shook, but it wasn't

enough. I was about to die from itchiness.

"The wagons, Phoebe! Run for the wagons! I'll run ahead for Happy Hawkins!"

I raced past the Flathead shacks. The Flathead woman didn't even look up. But the other O'Malleys did. By the time I made it back to our wagons I was trailing a passel of whooping, screaming redheads.

Amelia and Mama came running, brandishing cooking knives.

"What's going on?"

"Is there another bear?"

I sped past them straight into the arms of Happy Hawkins.

"Child! What've you done to yourself now?"

"Bugs!" was all I could yell.

Happy started stripping me, right then and there. When she finally noticed the gathering crowd, she hustled me into her wagon. And there I cowered, swatting and picking, till hot water and ointments and another dress were fetched.

When I finally emerged, the twins were still standing around, snickering.

"Where's tonight's steak dinner?"

"Or did you forget to take your rifle, Phoebe? What's the matter? Finally come up against something you can't handle?"

"How can a body handle fleas?" I spluttered.

"Why, la-de-da. You face 'em down like a herd of stampeding buffalo—"

"Or catch them right between the eyes like a jackrabbit—"

"Keep your peace, Hannah and Sarah," boomed an unexpected voice.

I spun around to find Miss Simpson standing there. A flicker of amusement turned up her lips. "Try and make some distance between yourself and the wildlife for a few more days, Phoebe. We're nearly to Oregon City."

"Yes, Miss Simpson. Thank you, Miss Simpson."

I slunk back to my family wagon.

ELEVEN

he entrance to the Barlow Road was tucked in the hills behind the Methodist Mission. We found the tollgate the next morning. It was a real wooden one, like on some roads back East, and it was manned by Mr. Samuel Barlow himself. Miss Simpson pulled her wagon up first and strode forth to bargain. It wasn't any use.

"Five dollars a wagon, ma'am. And ten cents each head of horse—loose, geared, or saddled."

"That's outrageous!"

"You spent the last year carvin' this road outten the wilderness, ma'am? Another ten cents for each head of horned cattle, whether geared or loose. And you better be payin' up fast. I'm fixin' on closin' her down for the winter."

"Why?"

"Snow's comin' on, is why. Can't keep 'er open after the snows come on."

We paid up.

"Shouldn't be too bad goin' as far as the Tygh Valley," Samuel Barlow offered as he opened the gate for Miss Simpson's wagon. "It's a mite steep pullin' out of that. You'll be all right, though, so long's you make the Barlow Pass afore the snows."

Miss Simpson didn't deign to answer, only whacked her oxen and plowed through. I had a question, though, as Amelia and I followed.

"What's the Barlow Pass, sir?"

"Why, that's at the highest point of the Cascade Mountains, miss. Leastways the highest point you can pull a wagon over. Dead south of Mount Hood, it is. Named it myself."

I'd thought as much. I nodded thanks and fixed my eyes on the bulk of Mount Hood that already towered ahead of us. Cold snow gleamed as the morning sun hit the mountain's eastern side.

I shivered. *Please, Lord. Let us make the pass before the snows.*

We did make it to the Tygh Valley before the snows. We even got out of the Tygh Valley, not much thanks to Mr. Samuel Barlow and his precious road. The truth about that road was soon all too evident. It wasn't much more than the worst of the tracks we'd been laboring along these long last months. Could it have been harder if we'd stayed along the Columbia and saved our money? We'd never have the answer to that one. In the here and now we forded endless creeks. We worked deeper and higher into the thickly forested mountains. And two mornings after we got out of the Tygh Valley we woke to a blanket of snow.

Papa crawled to the tailgate of the wagon, crutches foremost, to examine the latest calamity. He poked a crutch through the white stuff until it was tapping hard ground, then pulled out the stick to examine it.

"Could be worse. Only about six inches."

Amelia stared at Papa unbelievingly. "Back in Massachusetts, you treated six inches like a *blizzard*, Papa, even though we'd gotten far worse. You used to let the sheep huddle and take to the fireplace until the thaw."

"I don't appreciate your sense of exaggeration, Amelia." Papa peered up into the sky. The thick, milky swirl of clouds wasn't promising. "Think I'll just go see Miss Simpson. We ought to move right on out while the animals can still find their footing through this."

Papa lurched off and I caught Amelia's eye. "Papa's finally starting in, just like I figured he would."

"Miss Simpson can handle him, Phoebe." She shook snow from her blankets and began folding them. "I'm not so sure what she can do about the weather, though."

Mama was valiantly trying to kindle a spark in sodden logs. "We've less than seventy miles to safety, daughters. After surviving almost two thousand miles from Independence, Missouri, the Lord wouldn't desert us now. I am a little worried about the food supply, though. Phoebe's bear is gone, and I was only able to trade for a little salmon from those Flatheads. I pray it will keep us sustained."

The snow caught up with us again at our nooning. All the livestock were exhausted from pushing through it for the few miles we'd made that morning. But the gray heavens broke and more snow began to fall, thick and heavy. We packed up and struggled forward.

It was still snowing when darkness fell. It snowed all through the night. For the first time since Papa's accident, Mama shared quarters with Papa and the cherrywood dresser. For the first time since the trip began, Amelia and I joined them. Papa fussed less than I thought at the invasion of his territory. But then, he had no choice. Not if he wanted to continue in this life with a wife and two daughters.

The snow was almost two feet deep by morning.

We soldiered on, nevertheless. It kept falling, and a scant mile or two farther, Miss Simpson called a halt.

"I can't find the trail any longer. We'll have to stop, or we'll just get lost. We may already be lost."

It was the first time I saw defeat in Miss Simpson's shoulders. It was frightening. Together we'd braved buffalo disasters, Indian abductions, prairie fires, and even bears. After all that, none of us could believe mere snow could stop us. None of us could ever conceive of so much snow. Almost three feet, and still falling. Amelia touched my shoulder.

"What are we going to do, Phoebe?"

I brushed freezing flakes from my face and tried to pat some feeling back into my cheeks. Then I bent over to have a go at the toes poking from my worn-out boots. "We'll have to find some better kind of shelter, Amelia. The wagon's too cold, even with all of us crushed together. We'll have to dig in."

The digging-in part was almost fun, almost like frolicking in the snow when we were youngsters back home. Amelia and Mama and I chose a spot between one side of the wagon and the encroaching forest and began preparations for making a little cave out of the stuff. Mama measured off a small circular floor area and busied herself stomping it flat, while Amelia and I formed the snow into hard blocks about the size of building stones. Papa sat hunched by his window inside the wagon, calling out directives through the still-falling flakes.

"See you don't make those blocks so heavy you can't hoist them, daughters. . . . Not like that! Butt the first row right close to each other. The second row should alternate over the butting edges of the lower blocks. For strength . . . Shove that third row of blocks a few inches inward, so the roof can start coming together. Height's not called for in this enterprise."

It didn't take too long for our neighbors to get curious.

"What'cha doing, Phoebe?"

"Building a house, Timothy. A snow house."

"May I play too?"

"Build your own house, Timothy. Tell Margaret and Lizzie. It will be cozy to sleep in tonight."

Timothy trotted off, fascinated by the idea. The twins came next.

"Lands! Whatever are you about?"

Amelia stopped in midstride while transporting a huge block for the third layer. I was lugging the other half and could hardly even feel my frozen fingers beneath its weight. "Making a shelter, Hannah. Isn't it obvious?"

"Surely you're not planning on wintering here, Amelia?"

"No, Sarah." Thankfully, Amelia continued the last three feet to the growing wall and we set down the block to Papa's specifications. "We're not planning on wintering here. But if you ever expect to make eyes at another young man, you might consider building something for yourselves and your mother."

"Pooh," Hannah said. But her *pooh* didn't have its usual conviction. "It's but the middle of October. The sixteenth, to be exact. I checked with Miss Prendergast. There's bound to be a thaw. Snows like this aren't natural."

"Maybe not back East, Hannah," I countered, all the while nursing my frostbitten fingers under my arms. "But, then, we're not back East anymore, are we?"

The significance of my statement began to prey upon Sarah. She took on that swooning look I hadn't seen for months. Hannah shoved out a hand to grasp her. "We haven't time for your nonsense, sister. The Browns may have a point. It *is* still snowing. . . ."

The Kennans staggered off through a drift and Amelia and Mama and I kept building, slowly closing in the roof gap. The sixteenth of October. Barely a month past our last disaster. A lot had happened even since then. A bunch of new ideas had come to me that needed more thinking time. Lots more thinking time. I swiped at the flakes freezing to my eyelashes and continued packing loose snow carefully and methodically into the cracks between snow blocks. I intended to live long enough to get all the thinking time I needed.

In the morning I crawled out of our shelter to inspect the situation. More snow had fallen, but it wasn't snowing anymore. The sky still had that sullen look, though. It was the same kind of look Hannah and Sarah Kennan had had just after their rescue from the Pawnee, when they'd been none too pleased to be torn from the anticipated delights of marriage to Wind Pony and Panther Claw. It was a distinctly revengeful sort of sky.

With the air clear for the moment, though, I could finally make out where our party had landed. The wagons were strung out in an angled line heading uphill. The only clear spots to inspect the sky from this narrow corridor were either directly above, ahead of the wagons, or behind them. To either side we were hemmed in by snow-covered behemoths of the forest—giant firs and pines and other evergreens I hadn't even the ghost of a name for. Maybe Mr. Samuel Barlow had done some work on his road after all. Someone had cut this swathe through the ancient forest.

My attention drifted back to the earth before me. To the snow, to be more precise, for there certainly wasn't any earth to be seen. The night before we'd made a little path from our snowbound wagon to the entrance of our cave. I scuffed with disgust through the fresh foot of the stuff that had fallen on this passageway. The drift to either side was taller than I was. It was perfectly obvious nobody could haul wagons through five feet of snow.

There were shallow paths everywhere, like groundhog tunnels laid open to the sky. I followed along one, hoping to find signs of life somewhere. I stumbled onto the livestock first. We'd huddled all the stock together for warmth the afternoon before. When they caught sight of me they started in bawling and neighing, sending up a cloud of frozen breaths. Poor creatures. They were hungry and thirsty and confused. They were from the East too.

Since I was only upsetting them I gave up on the stock for the moment and pressed on. A few in our party had made caves like ours. Others had stuck to their wagons, reasoning that all the falling snow would cling to the canvas and create their own little caves. Now I passed the shrouded wagon mounds, not liking the heavy dips I saw in them. What would happen if the tired cloth gave out, smothering everything—and everyone—within?

The first human sound I heard came from a wagon just up ahead. It was a distinct groan, followed by a sharp screech. I sank my frozen toes into the nearest drift and fought my way through.

"Yoohoo! Who's in there?"

There was a sharp intake of breath before a voice panted out with effort. "The baby. My baby's coming!"

Holy smoke. Mrs. Hatch's baby! "Hang on, ma'am. I'll find Happy Hawkins!"

My first reaction was to barrel through that snowdrift in circles. Then I stopped and thought. It might take forever to figure out which drift Happy and her husband were tucked into. I opened my mouth and let out a shout.

"Hap-py! Happy Hawkins! The baby's coming and you're needed!"

I must have bellowed louder than I thought, but I did get results. The first was unexpected. My voice set off an avalanche of snow from the heavily laden fir trees overhead—right down onto the wagons, then onto me. I was nearly buried. But my head was still above water, so to speak. I shook myself and let out another yell. That was a tactical error. Another avalanche packed my neck solid. I swiveled it enough to make out figures popping from holes, blinking molelike in the harsh whiteness of the light. Happy must have been one of them, but I couldn't see that far. I heard her, though.

"Where's Mabel?"

"This way, Happy," I cried.

"Keep bellowing out till I set my sights on you, Phoebe."

"I can't! I'm getting smothered!"

"There you are. Leastways the top of your head. Hang on!"

Just in time Happy was hauling me out by my hair, then my armpits. She dusted me down and set me back on the path with no nonsense.

"Get a fire started right here, Phoebe." She turned away to bawl out: "Theodore! Find your shovel! I need this drift dug out to Mabel's tailgate!" Then she was back to me. "A big fire, Phoebe. Get the girls to find some wood under these drifts and start melting snow. I'll need boiling water."

"Yes, ma'am. Right away, ma'am."

I plowed off in the direction where Amelia and the other girls had begun to gather. Mabel Hatch's baby had certainly picked its moment.

It was a fine, strapping boy, just as Margaret had predicted. Thinking back on it all, maybe that baby *had* chosen the perfect moment to arrive. What Blizzard Hatch did was probably save our lives. He made the whole camp stop feeling sorry for itself and work together.

After we got that first fire going, it suddenly seemed obvious that we had to build others and begin melting snow to hand-water the livestock. With good drinks in them, the cattle and horses had more will to paw through the snow for forage. Since the ground cover was fairly well smothered, we had to chop down a few trees to keep the fires going. Inspecting the downed trees made it perfectly clear that extra fir and pine boughs could become soft mattresses for our snow caves.

One thing simply led to another and the day was gone. The snow started in again for a while just as darkness fell, but it didn't seem to have the same body to it, and didn't amount to much.

Our family was sitting on thick evergreen boughs by the fire just outside our cave opening. We were drinking the last of our coffee and eating the last of our salmon—the last of our food, period. I warmed my hands with the scalding coffee cup, savoring its warmth, loath to drink the final inch. But I wasn't unhappy.

"This was some day, wasn't it?" I thought aloud.

"Indeed it was, Phoebe." Mama's face softened as sounds of the new baby's hungry cries came through the still night air. He didn't cry for long.

"Mrs. Hatch must be feeding him again," Amelia offered. "The change that's come over her!"

"She's been smiling for hours," I broke in. "I never knew her to smile before. It makes her absolutely beautiful, even tired out like she is. And she actually let me touch the baby!"

"Doesn't he have some appetite, though. And what a romantic name!"

"*Blizzard*," Papa scoffed. "What kind of a tom-fool name is that for a healthy boy?"

"Blizzard *John*, Papa. The John is for his late father."

"Still and all, Phoebe—"

"I think it's the most wonderful name imaginable." Amelia waxed poetic. "What a hero he could grow into! Born in a blizzard in the middle of the Cascades. Raised up strong in the new country of Oregon . . . It's got the makings of an epic, at the least."

"You going to write it, Amelia? His make-believe story?" The question just slipped out of my mouth. Over the fire I caught one of Papa's eyebrows rising dramatically. Oh, dear. I'd best pull my foot out of my mouth fast. "In your head, I mean. A little good storytelling could keep us entertained right over the pass and down into Oregon City."

Amelia frowned. "Assuming we ever make it to the pass, Phoebe."

My sister's deep, dark literary secret was instantly forgotten. I swallowed the last of the coffee. I needed it to quell the abrupt chill in my stomach. " 'Course we'll make it to the pass!"

"I've got no intention of wintering here!" barked Papa.

"I'm sure we could make it cozy," Mama tried. She was attempting to look at the bright side of a hopeless situation. No matter how you considered it, five feet of snow was more than daunting. Five feet of snow could be neither plowed through nor wished away.

"Truly cozy. Only consider how much comfort the evergreen branches have already offered us." Mama kept skating over the thin ice of the catastrophe. Papa egged her on.

"Next thing you'll be trying to hang the girls'

skins up for a cave door, Ruth, and adding windows with curtains!"

"Why, I never thought you could come up with such homey suggestions, Henry!"

Amelia and I grimaced at each other across the fire. Poor Mama had been so long without a proper home, it was starting to affect her. She came back to earth fairly quickly, though.

"There is the matter of food, however. . . ."

Food. I rubbed my half-filled stomach. Five feet of snow without provisions was also the recipe for total disaster. No point in thinking about it. Maybe tomorrow . . .

I crawled away from the fire to curl up in the cave. My dispirited family followed.

TWELVE

The morrow was bright and bitterly cold. There'd be no more snow in the offing, but there wouldn't be any thawing this day, either. I stood blinking by the cave entrance, contemplating boiled snow for breakfast.

Hannah and Sarah Kennan slid by, intent on a mission, rifles aggressively clutched by their sides. Funny how they changed with rifles in their hands. There wasn't even a touch of mincing, prancing, waltzing, or swooning about them.

"Where you twins off to?"

"Hunting, Phoebe. There's got to be something to eat out there."

"Sure, Hannah. Wolves. Hear them howling all night?"

Hannah shook her head. "It's not wolves we're after, though I'd eat one of them, too."

She meant business. "Hold on a minute. I'll get my rifle and come with you."

"No, Phoebe," Sarah answered for both of them. "This is *our* duty. We discussed it and decided upon it. When our mama wakes, you may tell her where we've gone."

"But Sarah, Hannah, it would be safer if—" Too late. They were gone. I shook my head, then bent to rouse up the remnants of last night's fire.

"They did *what!*"

The camp was in almost as much of a tizzy as the day before when Blizzard John Hatch was being born. Miss Simpson had just discovered the absence of the Kennan twins.

"Why didn't you come to me with this information, Phoebe? Why didn't you come immediately?"

"Their minds were set, Miss Simpson. And I figured we could always track them by their footprints in the snow—"

"And how far are they going to get before they sink over their heads in some drift and suffocate?"

"There's a nice, crisp surface developing over the drifts, Miss Simpson, in case you hadn't noticed. A deft-footed person could nearly slide across the top—"

"It won't do, Phoebe. We'll have to get together a search party."

That was when I remembered a forgotten fact. "Wait a minute, ma'am. The twins this morning? They really were moving fairly fast, almost skimming. . . ."

I closed my eyes, trying to recollect the scene. "Snowshoes! They had snowshoes, Miss Simpson!"

Tabitha Kennan was wilting by the nearest fire. My comment perked her up some. "Of course! My dear departed George insisted on bringing several pair, just in case. . . ."

Happy Hawkins was rubbing her chin. "You packing any more snowshoes, Tabitha? Anyone else got some?" After the solid round of no's, Happy turned to Miss Simpson. "Why don't we give the twins a few more hours? In case they actually bag something."

"They have been amazingly resilient thus far, Emily," Miss Prendergast added.

Mr. Hawkins walked up to the group, working a few slim fir twigs in his hands. He'd left his hat somewhere and his bushy head of hair was almost as white as the snowdrifts. The bear-claw scars across one cheek added an incongruous touch of angry pink to his otherwise mild visage. "Can you boil up a pot of water for me, Happy? I'd like to heat these into shape for snowshoes." He glanced over to me. "Could you spare a few strips of elk skin for webbing, Phoebe? Get me some snowshoes, I can go after them."

"Yes, sir, Mr. Hawkins."

I went quickly to fetch the skin, but my heart wasn't completely in the gesture. Why hadn't I started in on that dress I'd been thinking about? Maybe because I hadn't truly had the nerve to cut into the skin. Maybe I'd been suspicioning it might also cut into the memory of Yellow Feather and his first sister. Now my prized possession was about to be marred. Were the Kennan twins worth it?

I kicked myself for the vile selfishness of the thought, but had a hard time getting it out of my mind nevertheless. Then I remembered my bear skin. Its pungent warmth had comforted the whole family last night. And I'd always have my blood-sister scar, till my dying day . . . which might be sooner than anticipated at the rate things were deteriorating. I guessed I could spare a little elk skin for the twins after all.

It took Mr. Hawkins a long time to make that pair of snowshoes. By late morning he was still laboriously weaving bits of webbing. Long before that I'd given up on Yellow Feather's elk skin ever turning into a dress. In fact, I'd given up as soon as Mr. Hawkins had trimmed off the strips he deemed necessary for his errand of mercy. I just sat there in the cold snow staring at the mutilated remains. Bending over to rub my freezing toes for about the thousandth time, I got the idea.

Moccasins. Most all of the Indians we'd met had

worn comfortable moccasins. Lined with bits of fur from the bear skin, my toes would be in heaven. Without further ado, I fetched Mama's sewing kit from her cherrywood dresser, pulled off a boot to trace my foot size on the hide, and set to work.

"Are those my good scissors, Phoebe?"

"Yes, Mama." Slumped over my work at foot level, I couldn't help but inspect Mama's boots. She hadn't done as much walking as Amelia and I, but her toes were poking out too. My eyes slid over to Amelia, who was tending our fire. Her toes were sticking out worse than mine. I sighed.

"You and Amelia give me a little advice here, Mama, maybe we can all warm up our feet. You two always did have better hands at needlework."

For our noon dinner we boiled elk-skin scraps into a little broth. With the last of our salt and pepper added it didn't taste that bad. Truly, it wasn't that much worse than dried buffalo jerky soup. The bits of hide were a mite chewy going down, however. Papa slurped his broth with no comment. Amelia swallowed hers thoughtfully.

"I never believed we'd be this hungry again. After the Kansas River I thought we couldn't *possibly* be as hungry again. Ever. Curiously, I'm not *that* hungry. But if the Kennan twins have no luck . . ."

"Yes, Amelia?" Mama wanted to know the answer to that one.

"Well, Mama . . . Phoebe sacrificed her precious elk skin today. I suppose it's only fair that my buffalo be next. Although I *was* wondering if there might be any food value in Indian trade beads. . . ."

Not even Papa bothered to answer that question. I moved uncomfortably on my seat of boughs, then shifted a hand to rearrange a hard lump. My fingers came up with a pine cone. As it jiggled on my palm, a seed fell out. I sniffed at the offering.

"Smells a little like turpentine. Still . . . you suppose these could be eaten?"

Four sets of eyes stared hungrily at the pine nut in my hand before Amelia made a dive for the cave. She emerged with another half-dozen cones. "I do sew better than you, Phoebe. You want to hunt for pine cones this afternoon, or shall I?"

Strange how the food had all run out again for everyone at the same time. Thinking about it, it made sense. We were meant to be in Oregon City by this time. Miss Simpson's Petticoat Party was a week or two behind schedule, and so were its supplies.

The camp was busy again that afternoon. Happy and Mr. Hawkins fussed over those snowshoes, Mama and Amelia stitched up a storm, and every other able body was sinking through drifts in the surrounding forest banging at pine trees for cones. The sun was setting before I even remembered the absent Kennan twins again. I was roasting a panful of pine nuts over the fire, salivating at the smell. My stomach lurched as the thought hit me.

How could they find their way back from wherever they'd been in the dark? And if they didn't manage that, how could Hannah and Sarah survive the night in the forest?

I glanced away from the bright fire to focus into the deepening gloom of the surrounding woods. None of us had ventured after our pine nuts more than a hundred feet from the trail today. The trees had closed in too tightly, too smotheringly— blocking off the distant sky, frightening us.

Even with the aid of their snowshoes, it was suddenly hard to visualize Hannah and Sarah safely negotiating what was surely a more formidable expanse of wilderness beyond. Would we ever see them again?

I had to pull the pan from the fire before I spilled its precious contents. I set it down and grabbed at my stomach.

"What's the matter, Phoebe?"

Mama looked up from the last few stitches she was giving my new moccasins. She'd double-lined them. Elk on the outside, buffalo on the inside. And she'd made them long, so they'd reach nearly to my knees. They were going to be very special.

"Has that elk-skin soup upset you?"

"It's not that, Mama." But I was still hanging on to my stomach, when maybe it should've been my heart. Matching golden braids and pert noses and *la-de-das* swept through my head. Remorse lodged there, too—a little for my growing envy of their ripe looks, but more for begrudging them shooting skills I knew I'd never match. "It's just that Hannah and Sarah . . . It's too late for Mr. Hawkins to go after them, isn't it?"

Mama finished the last stitch and carefully bit off the thread. She inspected her fingers, which were red from the cold and sore from pushing her needle through the tough hide. "I've never worked with leather before. It's very different from cotton or silk."

Amelia glanced up from her own boots. Even in the dying light I could tell that her eyes were damp. She swiped at her nose with the edge of her shawl. "Miss Simpson should have let them marry Wind Pony and Panther Claw back in Pawnee country. At least they'd be alive. They'd probably even be happy."

Papa was holed up in the snow cave rather than

the wagon, but we could still hear his voice. "Never!" The word echoed and reverberated. "A fate worse than death! Captain Kennan would have turned in his—"

"He wouldn't have, you know, Henry," Mama interrupted. "And he wouldn't have climbed out of it, either. We're all different now. We're tougher. I'd rather know that my daughters had survived . . . through whatever means necessity dictated."

Necessity. I snuffled and slung the pine nuts back over the fire. Some of us were going to make it. We'd make it even if we had to eat every pine nut in the Cascades. Even if we had to abandon our wagons and walk out over the pass to Oregon City and the Willamette Valley.

It wasn't a very cheerful supper. We sat crunching the nuts. We ate them one by one, trying to make a handful last, trying to make believe those pine nuts and hot melted snow were filling our stomachs.

Slowly the sounds of the night surrounded us. There were the livestock, finally settling into silence after moaning pitifully most of the day. The O'Malleys had managed to get a little milk from their cow. They'd divided it among Timothy and the smallest girls, but the lion's share went to

Mabel Hatch so she could nurse her baby. If the thaw didn't start in the morning . . . In case the thaw didn't come, I knew there were contingency plans. I'd heard Miss Simpson and the Hawkinses making them.

"Well, it's fairly obvious," Miss Simpson had said. "We'll have to slaughter one of the animals, before they start to die on us anyway. Or the wolves get them. We'll choose the weakest one first."

Happy and Mr. Hawkins had shrugged agreement. It made a certain amount of sense, but no one was overjoyed by the prospect. It signaled failure, complete and unequivocal.

So much for the livestock. Now the other night sounds swept over me. The wolves had started their howling again. They seemed to be coming in closer, circling us. Would they make a try at the weakened stock tonight? Make their killing before we did? Then there was baby Blizzard demanding his supper. His was easier to come by, at least for the moment. There were other sounds too. I swallowed my last nut and set down my plate. I raised my head.

"Hear anything, Amelia? Mama?"

Even Papa stopped crunching for a moment. "Just the wind coming up. That bear skin and buffalo robe will feel good tonight."

My head was still cocked. "It's more than that, Papa. It sounds almost like footsteps. Human footsteps."

Amelia's tin plate fell from her lap, scattering her last few precious nuts. "Is it possible?"

I was already on my feet and past the fire. I was in such a hurry I didn't even stop to notice how good and warm the new moccasins felt on my feet and legs.

"Hallo out there! Hannah! Sarah?" I sped past the rest of the camp only to stop short.

Emerging from the forest were unexpected faces. Indian faces.

THIRTEEN

he Indians, swathed in heavy blankets, filed silently toward the nearest fire. There were maybe half a dozen before the surprise. The surprise was another two braves weighed down by a deer slung between them from a long pole.

And following the deer, sneaking up just as quietly as the Indians had, were the Kennan twins.

"Hannah!" I gasped. "Sarah! You're alive!"

"La-de-da, Phoebe." Hannah grinned. "What were you expecting?"

Tabitha Kennan hurried up, took one look at the Indians and her daughters, and swooned. Luckily Miss Simpson and Happy Hawkins were not far behind. Miss Simpson caught Mrs. Kennan and passed her on to Happy. "You deal with her, Happy. I don't think I'm up to it."

Happy wasn't either. In a moment Mrs. Kennan was forgotten in Mrs. Davis's lap, and the remainder of the Petticoat Party was gawking at our unexpected visitors.

"Miss Simpson." This time Sarah spoke. "Miss

Simpson, I'd like to present to you Lu-Kut-Chee. He's the chief of these Chinook Indians. Wasn't it fortunate Hannah and I bumped into them?"

For once Miss Simpson was wordless.

Hannah obligingly filled the gap. "Sarah and I were tramping around forever, it seemed like, and only got one skinny squirrel." She lifted her cloak and exhibited the sorry, frozen bundle.

"That's when we saw the hoof marks in the snow," Sarah continued. "So sister and I tracked those marks neat as you could please—"

"Until we saw the buck," finished Hannah. "He wasn't expecting us." She raised her rifle barrel. "*Boom*. There was nothing to it. Except then we discovered our buck was a little weightier than we'd anticipated." She gestured toward the animal. "A six-point rack. Wouldn't our daddy be pleased?"

Miss Simpson gurgled, as if she might be getting back the use of her vocal cords again.

Sarah Kennan didn't give her a chance to make the test. "So Hannah and I thought, well, we'd best just stay by our booty for a while. Someone was sure to come and help us—"

"And they did!" Hannah squealed. "Just the nicest bunch of Indians we've met yet." The firelight was bright enough to show the adoration in her eyes as she turned to Lu-Kut-Chee. "Tell our friends what you gentlemen were doing wandering around in the mountains, Lu."

Lu-Kut-Chee made a motion to the braves still hoisting the deer, and they let it drop, pulling out knives to begin the butchering. "We find *Boston Klootchman—*"

"That means American women," Hannah interrupted. "*Boston* is 'American,' and *Klootchman—*"

"Do be civil enough to allow the chief to finish his thoughts, Hannah," Miss Simpson snapped. She'd found her lost voice, sure enough.

The Indian chief almost smirked. "We find *Boston Klootchman* on journey to Dalles for trade. Chinook best traders. Good English. Good many tongues. Never get lost, even in snow." He rubbed his hands together briskly. "Have 'bacca to warm while meat *mamook piah muckamuck?*"

"I think Lu means have we any tobacco to smoke while the meat cooks," Hannah translated.

"I believe I understood what he meant, Hannah." Miss Simpson studied the gathering. "Mr. Hawkins, did you not once smoke a pipe?"

"I did, but the 'baccy's all gone." He turned to Mrs. Davis, who was patting Tabitha Kennan's cheeks. "Your Arthur enjoyed a chew now and then, didn't he, Mildred?"

"Dear me, so he did." She dropped Mrs. Kennan

from her lap to stand. "There may still be a small cache tucked away."

The gathering shifted from one cold foot to another somewhat uncomfortably in Mrs. Davis's absence. Hannah removed the scarf wrapping her head, allowing Lu-Kut-Chee to openly admire the glints of gold the fire cast on her hair, while Sarah bent over one of the braves working on the deer carcass. This one was obviously *her* choice.

"Sarah, get over here at once!"

"Goodness, Miss Simpson, I was only seeing if Kim-Tah needed any assistance."

Sarah rose as Mrs. Davis returned with several twists of tobacco. The braves gathered around for their shares and the deer was forgotten.

"Phoebe?"

I started at the voice from behind me. "Yes, Mama?"

"I brought knives. If we wish to dine better this evening, I suspect we must get the meal on the fire ourselves."

"You're probably right, Mama."

That one buck fed the entire camp—Indians included—that night. I found out later that Mama had hidden a full haunch of it for the next day. She was right in doing that, too. Those Chinooks had appetites as good as any Sioux I ever met. Funny thing about Indians. They'd eat up anything set before them, in whatever quantity. They wouldn't stop eating till it was all gone, either.

But the meat was gone by and by. Cleaning his teeth with a bone toothpick, Lu-Kut-Chee himself searched the fires for more. When he was satisfied it was good and finished, he settled back by the biggest fire on folded legs and pulled out his tobacco and pipe for a comfortable smoke. He did that different from the Sioux, though.

The smoke curling into the night air took me back to Scotts Bluff and Arrow Shield the medicine man making his offerings to the Great Spirit. Yellow Feather's father, Black Tail of Hawk, and the other Sioux had used tobacco as part of their religion. Lu-Kut-Chee must have spent too much time trading with white men. The only magic left in the smoke was the satisfaction the smoking seemed to give him.

After he and his men had finished with that, they began wrapping themselves into their blankets. Miss Simpson made a try at talking weather and the Barlow Pass with them, but they'd have nothing to do with her. When it was time to eat, they'd eaten. Now it was time to sleep. They slept.

Miss Simpson shook her head. "Men." She

began waving everyone else off to their own bur-
rows, then had a final thought. "Hannah and
Sarah? You'll be sharing my quarters tonight. Your
mother, too."

"But—"

"Miss Simpson—"

"No buts about it. I have spoken."

A drip woke me in the morning. It came from
the ceiling of the snow cave above, right smack
onto my forehead.

Plop . . . plip . . . plip-plip, plop.

I brushed off the moisture and lay there a few
moments until the significance of the water hit me.
Then I bolted upright, banging my head into the
low roof.

"It's melting!" I yelled.

"Pipe down and let a man get his sleep,
Phoebe." Papa rolled over.

I ignored him. "The temperature's rising! A
thaw's coming on!"

Amelia and Mama poked their heads out from
under the skins.

"Gracious," Mama murmured. "The Lord has
remembered us."

I flew from the cave.

We'd slept late. The sun was high. There was a

soft wind blowing from the west, and little rivulets of water were flooding our beaten paths.

"Saved! We're saved!" I just had to yell some more. I would have danced, too, but my feet were still bare. I crawled back inside for my new moccasins. Finally fully dressed, I ran out to spread the joyous news.

Miss Simpson already knew. She was consulting with Lu-Kut-Chee over her fire. She nodded at me, but chose not to impart her newly gleaned information until a goodly number of the party surrounded her. Finally she spoke.

"It's a 'chinook' wind we're feeling. It's named after our Indian friends, or vice versa. At any rate, it blows warm and is good news, indeed." Miss Simpson actually smiled. "The other good news is that we're barely a mile from the Barlow Pass. The snows are nowhere near as heavy on the other side. We have only to thaw for a day or two before moving on."

Lu-Kut-Chee held up a cautionary hand.

"Yes?"

"Do not wait long. More snow comes. *Cole illahee*—winter—be *peshak*, bad." He sniffed the wind and studied the sky. "Ver' bad in mountains this winter." The chief fastened his snowshoes and slung his blankets around his body. His braves shouldered their packs and followed his gestures.

My attention shifted to the Kennan twins. Hannah and Sarah were only now figuring out that their Indians were leaving.

"Lu-Kut-Chee!"

"Kim-Tah!"

Their wails were heartrending. Even the braves were touched. Lu-Kut-Chee's taut features softened. "My name means 'clam.' When clams come from sand in great water, when spring comes, I return. Find *Boston Klootchman* with hair of gold. Good shot. Make good squaw."

Kim-Tah grunted. That apparently meant he had similar plans in mind for Sarah.

The twins beamed. Mrs. Kennan took a while to work out the discussion before swooning again. Nobody caught her as she plopped into a fresh rivulet.

Nobody caught Tabitha Kennan because we were all staring at Miss Simpson, waiting for her response to the most recent proposal for the twins' hands. Not that it was an actual formal proposal. There hadn't even been any horses offered. No, it was more on the order of an assured assumption.

Miss Simpson considered for a long minute before shrugging her broad shoulders expressively. "That's as it may be. Hannah and Sarah will be off my conscience by then. In the meantime"—she held out a hand to the chief—"we thank you kindly for your assistance."

Lu-Kut-Chee ignored the offered hand but nodded gravely. He set off down the trail toward the east. His braves followed.

I watched them disappear from sight until someone snickered behind me. "Margaret? What's so funny?"

"Heaven help me, Phoebe." She let out a guffaw. "For I surely can't help myself!" She grabbed her stomach as a peal of laughter erupted. "That one, that chieftain with the huge nose and the huge mouthful of a name . . ."

I smiled as I began to catch on.

"Such a name, Phoebe, and all it means . . ." Her laugh was near to killing her. "All it means, in sum, is . . ."

I swiped at my tearing eyes.

"*Clam!*" we roared out together.

Hannah made a ferocious scowl. I poked Margaret.

"What do you suppose *Kim-Tah* might mean?"

We doubled over, aching with glee and relief.

FOURTEEN

*M*ama hauled the frozen venison joint from its snowbank before noon. The sorry little squirrel turned up along with it. None complained as Mama proceeded to roast the meat and make a soup from the squirrel. They knew by this time it would be share and share alike for everyone in the party.

All that day and the next we busied ourselves with making repairs to our wagons and trying to force as much water as possible into the livestock. That last effort was based on the theory that if an ox's stomach was sloshing with water it might forget there wasn't any grass mixing around with it. The stock was weakening fast, but wasn't hopeless. Not yet.

By the third morning after the Chinooks departed, enough snow had melted for us to try to move on. Lu-Kut-Chee's words about not lingering came back to me as Amelia and I yoked up Buck and Bright. The narrow strip of sky lay above us, a tunnel through the forest between our past and our future. And that patch of sky was clouding over ominously again. I sniffed the wind the way the Chinooks had.

"Notice a difference, Amelia?"

Amelia knotted her shawl. "The wind's not warm anymore, Phoebe. And the melt is beginning to turn to ice."

"Exactly. Thank goodness we're leaving."

"If Buck and Bright can manage." Amelia patted the nearest bony flank. "We know you're hungry, boys. We are too. But there's grass ahead."

"Lots of grass," I added in encouragement. Buck licked his nose and gave me one of his sad, weary, trusting looks.

Ahead, the first wagon lurched into movement.

We actually got to see the cone of Mount Hood that day—the cone that had been hidden by mist and snow since the Tygh Valley. It was from the top of the Barlow Pass that we saw it. We knew it had to be the pass, because spread out below were several miles of valley. *That* was Summit Meadows, for breaking through the snow-covering were patches of grass. Green grass. Even with the sky cleared momentarily for a stunning view of Mount Hood, no one was paying that view much attention. All eyes were riveted on the grass.

"Can you see it, Buck? Can you smell the *food* down there?"

He must have, and Bright and the other oxen too. Without even waiting to be nudged, they lumbered off down the pass to their dinners.

Not only did we noon in Summit Meadows, we lay over for the remainder of the day, as well. We'd only made about three miles, but there was no way the animals would be moved from their feast. We didn't even consider trying. I gave Papa a hand getting out of the wagon for some needed exercise, then reached back in for the family rifle.

"You have something in mind, daughter?"

"I don't have to help Mama with the dinner, since there's nothing left to cook. I think I saw some tracks in the snow, though. What I had in mind was finally doing Mr. Harley proud."

Papa shook his head doubtfully as he eased onto his crutches. "Didn't those Kennan girls just traipse off with their own weapons? Won't be much left to shoot with them on the hunt."

"Thank you for your confidence in me, Papa. However, I had no intention of playing second best to the twins."

I set off in something of a temper. What remained for me to do to prove myself? So the twins could shoot better. What about those cliffs

I'd scaled, and the grizzly I'd done in? Those twins hadn't shot any raging grizzly single-handed. I *was* going to bag something for the pot. Papa might complain about its being tough or stringy, but he'd not turn down his portion when it was time to eat.

I was so wound up I almost didn't notice when my footprints crossed those of the Kennan twins. I collected myself long enough to make for the opposite direction. Even I realized there was no point whatsoever in trying to compete on their hunting grounds. Instead, I headed for the far southwestern slope of the meadow, off where the dark mass of forest waited in brooding silence.

I slowed as I came closer to the trees, and began to pay attention to the signs around me, the way Mr. Harley had suggested. There were signs, too: splayed bird tracks, rodent prints. A drama. I plopped down in about a foot of snow and worked out the story.

It must have been a mouse. He'd risen from an underground burrow to check the air. . . . Searching more closely, I could just make out minuscule furrows tunneling helter-skelter under the fallen snow. There must be hundreds of mice down there.

This one had been unlucky. He'd popped from

his hole, wiggled his whiskers, unwisely decided the coast was clear, then begun scampering.

The tracks were tiny. I bent till my nose almost touched the snow. Four toes in front, five in the hind legs. He wasn't totally stupid, though. He'd zigged and zagged for several yards, till suddenly—*swoop!* The tracks ended.

I crawled over to the spot and picked up a soft tuft of white feather. An owl? Done in by an owl.

I began to notice other mappings across the snow. The most interesting were swishy brush marks heading for the forest nearby. Had someone taken a whisk broom to the snow? I sat back on my haunches, considering. Still considering, I carefully loaded the rifle. Next, I eased up to follow those whisks, right into the woods.

I had to stop and blink inside the cover of the trees. When my eyes readjusted themselves to the gloom I picked up the brush marks. Slowly but surely they made for a giant fir.

My eyes raised up along its trunk. There was a steady pattern of tooth marks. My creature was eating its way up the bark!

Without thinking, I cocked the rifle, raised the barrel, and followed the marks. They stopped short on a fat, furry blob.

I pulled the trigger.

←《》→

"A porcupine? How in blazes do you cook a porcupine? How do you *eat* a porcupine?"

"Gratefully, Henry," Mama responded. She already had our biggest pot over a blazing fire. The smile she gave me was glorious.

"I did try for a rabbit, Mama. But there weren't any rabbit tracks. I'll bet even Mr. Harley couldn't have found any rabbit tracks out there—"

"Mr. Harley would be proud of you, too, Phoebe. You'll have to remember, dear. When he gave you all that advice about hunting rabbits back at Laramie?"

"Yes, Mama?"

"Well, dear, I believe it was meant somewhat metaphorically. He really wanted you to understand the *concept* of hunting. . . ."

I began to get the idea. "That means I could substitute any creature for a rabbit, doesn't it? Except not my bear, since I wasn't exactly hunting after *her*."

"Yes, dear, it does." Mama beamed again, even while sucking at the finger one of Mr. Porcupine's quills had just pierced.

"Then this *is* Mr. Harley's rabbit. Tracked and cornered, fair and square. At last!"

Amelia finished packing snow into the pot and

straightened up. "The twins just waltzed by with three strapping jackrabbits. *Not* the metaphorical kind. Lizzie O'Malley got one too. I believe I'll take my turn with the rifle this afternoon, Phoebe."

I didn't pay Amelia one bit of attention. I was satisfied with my porcupine. Mr. Harley would've been too.

It was snowing again in the morning, but it hadn't amounted to much yet, so we pushed on. By the time we made Laurel Hill, the snow had changed to a fine, drizzling rain. And there we spent the remainder of the day, sloshing through mud as we snubbed our wagons to trees and one by one sent them down the Laurel Hill chute.

This was the biggest, meanest drop we'd yet met on the entire Oregon Trail. It was even worse than Windlass Hill, way back before Fort Laramie. But we were only forty miles from Oregon City, and nothing was going to stop us now.

At least Papa didn't have to ride down that chute on his back inside the wagon. Healed enough to be a little help, he and gentle Mr. Hawkins did a fair amount of cussing that day. We females didn't have the breath for any of that. We merely shouldered the load and got the work done.

During the next few days we forded a bunch of

creeks and the Clackamas River. It was a steady descent out of the Cascade Mountains, and as the forests thinned out, the land became rolling and greener still.

It kept raining. Amelia had taken to serious sneezing. Now she did it so hard, she almost spooked the oxen.

"God bless you, Amelia."

Snuffle. "Thank you, Phoebe."

"I've figured out why Oregon is so green, Amelia."

My sister didn't seem overwhelmed by curiosity. She sneezed again while I enlightened her. "*Gee*, Buck. *Gee!* . . . It's because it's always raining."

"Brilliant, Phoebe." Another sneeze erupted.

"God bless you twice." I sighed and continued tramping through the mud. So much for clever conversation on the trail. So much for inspiring feats of storytelling. The last few miles had degenerated into the endless mud of the beginning of our journey. Our minds must be falling apart with it. All we had left was the will to arrive.

Where *was* the end of the trail? Would we ever meet it? And what might transpire when we did? I hadn't wasted a lot of energy thinking about that up till now. Surviving had seemed sufficient. Just making it to the end of the Oregon Trail had become an end in itself.

It happened when we least expected it.

Our wagon was leading the party that morning. Of a sudden, the Barlow Road came to a dead stop before a sharp right turn. Sharp right turns were rare. They were also hard for oxen to manage. Amelia and I halted our team and walked forward to consider our next maneuver. Beyond the road was the edge of a cliff.

"Amelia?" By this time we had both worked past a thin screen of trees and were almost tottering on the brink of the precipice.

"Amelia? Could *that* be Oregon City?"

Amelia sneezed.

Margaret and Lizzie O'Malley were at our shoulders in a moment, and then the Kennan twins.

"Why in the world did you stop, Phoebe?"

"Saints above, is *that* Oregon City?"

Below us, hunkered down right at the base of the cliff, was a village of buildings. Real buildings, made of wooden slats painted white. I started to count them.

"Six, eight, ten, fourteen, twenty . . ."

Margaret interrupted when I'd gotten past

forty. "There must be almost a hundred buildings. If you count some of those little ones that look like outhouses. It's not bad. Still . . . for this Da dragged us across three thousand miles from New York?"

"There *is* the river winding right past," Amelia tried. "And what seems to be a series of water-falls . . . and they're quite cheerful little houses. . . ."

"A church!" Mama had joined us. Her eyes picked out a second steeple. "Where there are churches, there must be civilization!"

"Praise the Lord!" Happy Hawkins threw in.

Amelia sneezed again. This time Papa blessed her. "Would you look at all that green land spreading out across the river?" His voice had the same awe in it as Mama's had when noticing the steeples. "Miles and miles of it! That must be the Willamette Valley!"

"Watch where you poke your crutches, Papa. You don't want to fall over the cliff now."

Papa backed off from the edge. "Thank you for your consideration, Phoebe."

"Well." Miss Simpson finally huffed up. Her glance below was short and sharp. "Well. It seems we women managed it after all."

A genuine smile broke across her stern features, softening them momentarily. Then she remembered her duty as leader of the Petticoat Party. "Phoebe

and Amelia? It's high time you moved your wagon.
You're blocking the way to the Promised Land!"

The Promised Land? . . . I considered carefully
as I followed Miss Simpson's orders a final time.
Well, why not? It was green enough for Papa, and
there were churches and the trappings of civilization for Mama. There seemed to be plenty of room
for Amelia and me to spread our wings and grow.

I slapped Buck's flanks.

"*Gee*, boy! Can't you smell that grass waiting for
you? It could just be tall enough for an elephant.
There might even be a few elephants hiding in it for
us to see. At least wonders as big as—"

Buck didn't wait on the rest of my thoughts. He
jerked into motion, pulling Bright and Amelia and
me and our wagon with him.